THE DEVIL AND THE DEEP

AND OTHER TALES

CHRISTIAN FRANCIS

A special thank you to two people who both were invaluable in helping this book come to be; Laura Hubner, who taught *Fairytale and Gothic Horror* on my Master's degree, and inspired me to start this whole writing journey. David W. Adams for giving me the push I needed to complete this book.

***

E-book: 978-1-916582-52-1
Paperback: 978-1-916582-53-8
Hardcover: 978-1-916582-54-5

***

Always for you Vicky xxx
- CF

STYLISTIC WARNING

The author would like to preface his book with a quick note about some aspects of the writing within:

- Your grammar experience may differ from that of the author.
- The use of head-hopping (multiple POVs) is a stylistic choice, and will happen more as the plot's pace increases. This is wholly intentional, and not a mistake.
- Dialogue tags are used freely, and without constraint.
- Commas can, and will be used as a breath within sentences.
- The author does not capitalise the word 'god' unless it's at the start of a sentence.

- The author is a firm believer in the preservation of the creative voice within fiction, and thus published *Anti Rule: Navigating The Lies About Fiction Writing*. This was to combat all the 'rules of writing' that some try to force upon writers, telling them they *have* to do things one way, or they will fail. This book, as with all of the author's books, was proudly written unbridled to those rules. If you *are* a believer in the rules that say that no book should have a prologue, or you should only use the 'said' dialogue tag, or you must 'show' not 'tell', then put this book down. It is not for you.
- This story is intended to be a short, fun read, akin to the pulp horrors of the 70s and 80s. That is all.

CONTENT WARNING

The author would like to advise readers of the following aspects that may trigger:

- Violence.
- A lot of grim, grim description.
- Lighthouses. *(You never know, that may be a trigger to some people)*

Contents

Other tales

When shadows whisper and the sea churns, the Abyss shall yield its darkest spawn into the light.

Eyes blind, yet see all, will witness as Dagon rises as the seventh blade strikes the holy vessel.

Veins of the world shall weep at his coming, as the air carries the scent of the dead.

He who slumbers in the deep shall awaken, and his dominion over the salt and storm shall herald an age of despair.

Look to the seas for his sign, as old as time, as inevitable as fate.

— DARK PROPHECIES

PROLOGUE

12th December 1975

"You lie to yourself, priest!" The words spilling out of the girl's mouth were laced with bitterness and hate. Her voice, twisted to speak the words of its puppet master, now clearly exposed the corruption within her, the vileness of the unwelcome invader that had poisoned her soul.

The last five hours in this stone room had been arduous. The familiar calls from the priest, direct from the scriptures he held, all seemed now to be futile. Each one of his holy demands had done nothing but make this night bleaker. What had been merely a child screaming obscenities now became an intellectual attack straight from a demon's mind.

"You like to think that your god created me," came the guttural words from the innocent girl's mouth. "And just because you can chain me," she continued. "You believe that you and your order hold dominion over me." Her words floated on the sulfuric stench in the air, to the priest's ears. He tried to ignore them. He tried to focus on the holy scriptures he held.

The coldness of this windowless, stone-lined room burrowed deep into the priest. His hands felt numb as he turned the pages of the book. His whole body ached in this subterranean chamber. But it was not just the cold that sent a reverberating chill down Father Michael Nádasdy's spine, but it was also being in the presence of this girl with a demonic voice. The very core of this priest's being tried to scream at him to run, to leave, and to never, ever return. Yet he also knew the battle was too great and came at too high a cost if he failed. He had to try to save the girl.

Chained to an altar in the middle of this large, dimly lit chamber, all that the monster could do was to shout insults and hurt the body it dwelled in. So it screamed and shouted and clawed, bit, and tore at its own skin, all as the holy man spoke the words he had been taught to recite.

"*Do you think you own me, you fettered abortion?*" the girl grimaced with glee as she suddenly yelled in a torment.

Ignoring the outburst, and despite the constant tendrils of doubt wrapping around him, Father Michael still persisted in his cause, determined. He had to succeed. But as he peered up and met the gaze of the beast, he knew full well that nothing had changed. This thing had as firm a grip on its host as it ever had, and all the hours of exorcism rites, lashes with holy water, commands on behalf of his chosen god, all the monster did was let out a sinister chuckle.

This girl's grin grew wider as a trickle of fresh blood crawled over her thin lips, brought on from her, biting her own tongue. And with her teeth now on full display, the malevolent joy her host felt was palpable.

"You have no power," she said, as her voice dipped into a guttural whisper.

Father Michael glanced again at the pages of the book in his hand. He blocked out the child's words as he scanned the Latin letters before him. But he could not shake the fact that he felt like a fool. The sacred words he spoke from the hidden volume of *The Rituale Romanum* were impotent against this force. Those words had been the secret weapon for all in his position and had proven unbeatable in the face of evil. Today though, he may have well been reading aloud a cookery book, the effect it had.

"You like to believe that my kind were born in fire," the girl continued. "You like to believe me to be a demon. A devil. A cursed being that once sat angelic. You, for some reason, believe that your god created all. They are your teachings, are they not?" The glee in her words slipped as she noticed the priest closing his eyes, not giving her the full attention she craved.

"*Priest!*" the demon screamed without the mask of the girl's voice. A guttural, angry boom that was enough to shock Father Michael into being dragged back into the moment, away from his internal doubts. "*Listen to me!*" it said.

Like a switch flipped, the monstrous voice cut away as the girl's young tones resumed, along with the rhetorical conversation, like it never missed a beat. "If your master created all, and if we were created by him, then you are punishing us for his mistake, meaning he... is fallible. Is that not proof that the very foundation of your belief is a lie?" Having stated her point, the girl glanced down and regarded the gouges on her thin arms, along with the self inflicted bites and scratches that were stained with dried blood. She looked at the metal cuffs that chained her to the stone altar she sat on.

"What do you want?" Father Michael asked with a tremble in his voice.

"You think that your sky-god has jurisdiction." Her voice dropped in pitch slightly as she spoke, almost to a whisper. "I will show you how wrong you are, and I will rain down the very hell you fear upon your world."

"You cannot exist," he said, as he masked his fear as best he could. "The one god you speak of *will* destroy you."

Looking at him in amusement, the girl's smile opened, showing her bloodied teeth. "*One* god? That is priceless. You cannot see the truth." she spoke as her voice got deeper. "How funny... But I shall give you my eyes to see."

In an instant, the girl's demeanor shifted, and a primal ferocity distorted her features. The clanking of chains accompanied the horrifying spectacle as her fingers ruthlessly sought out her own eye sockets. Before the priest could scream for her to stop, the girl's fingers were already embedded into her own small eyes. Without a second to pass, her fingers curled as she clawed out her own eyeballs, and blood spewed down her cheeks. This was an unholy onslaught, that the priest had no time to stop.

Then all of a sudden, a fresh scream emitted from her mouth, but it was not that of the demon's, but her real, childlike voice. A distraught cry from deep inside of her soul.

"No!" Father Michael shouted in a panic, as he dropped his holy book to the floor. But before he could get round the altar to her, the door behind him flung open, the wood almost cracking off its hinges, as it swung with incredible force.

"Petra!" the burly man shouted as he barreled through the door and ran past the priest to his daughter's aid.

In an instant, as the man arrived, the girl's screams became a horrific, victorious laugh.

"*Don't touch her, Joe!*" the priest cried out in vain. "*You have to stay away!*"

But it was too late.

"Petra, my baby!" The father cried again as he

tried to subdue his daughter's violence, grappling with her to stop her self-abuse. But he was powerless against this creature. Her gleeful, bloodied mouth could not stop its laughter as she ripped her eyeballs out of her head, tearing them from their stalks.

This girl, now reveling in her bloodied insanity, reached up her hands as her father weakly tried to wrestle control. She presented her grotesque offering to the horrified priest standing in front of the altar; The eyeballs, torn from their sockets, raised in a macabre salute to Father Michael Nádasdy. A twisted invitation to witness the impending chaos.

"Watch as I drown your god, priest!" she laughed.

"Petr-!"

Her father could not finish the words he tried to shout, as the girl opened one of her hands, let the fleshy remnants slime off her palm, and grip his face across the eyes.

Then... there was a stillness.

The two remained frozen for a few seconds as Father Michael stared helplessly.

The girl's eyeless, bloody, maniacal face turned to her father, her hand still upon him. His expression, one of shock, was frozen still, like his body.

Though Father Michael could have sworn it lasted longer, it lasted only for a moment. A moment where the priest felt his god leave this room. His once unwavering faith now faltered as he felt suddenly all alone. Abandoned. Left to hang.

When that short moment ended, a high-pitched, terrifying giggle escaped her father's mouth.

The girl then turned to the priest.

"Run, priest, *RUN!*" the demon from within her shouted, as her father then turned, still giggling under his breath. His eyes then suddenly turned to that of pure hate, as his grin dropped to a grimace.

The stone room, suspended in a brief stillness, had witnessed the grotesque twisting of her father's mind into something maniacal and feral.

"*Run!*" she shouted again.

Father Michael Nádasdy could not remember leaving. He could not remember seeing the two robed men tied up in the antechamber, screaming at him. He could not remember barreling up the stone steps into the main chapel.

He felt shock as he ran outside the building and into the derelict graveyard, as a snowstorm hit him with full force. He had forgotten about the storm that began when he arrived in the late hours of the night before. But it was here and present, battering him just as it battered the small town.

His only thought was that he had to get to the glove box in his car. He had no other choice.

As he fumbled with the keys, he heard angry screams approaching.

Glancing over his shoulder, he saw the father speeding out of the door and through the storm after him. Behind him, he was soon joined by the two robed men from the antechamber, now untied, all in the same maniacal trance. All carrying the same monstrous and murderous looks; as hateful as each other, as unnaturally cruel as each other.

They all wailed, their voices merged into a cacophony of malice, echoing over the sounds of the turbulent weather, as they sprinted towards the priest, wanting nothing more than to destroy him.

Finally finding his key, and at the threshold of his own existential abyss, Father Michael unlocked, then opened his car door. Scrambling, he clicked open the glove box and removed the gun that lay within.

"Lord, forgive me."

ONE

17 Years Later

The summer months had brought an unseasonable chill upon the small fishing town of Port Gaynor. Icy rain had pelted it into submission for the past week, causing most residents to stay indoors. Winds had relentlessly battered their houses with their bluster, and the clouds had blotted out the sun's warmth for days.

On the west of this town stood St Jude's church. Not a grand building, to say the least, but a functional one for those of any faith. The building had not been looked after for many years, and showed signs of its aging. There were slight cracks in the walls, missing roof slates, and it was overgrown with ivy tracing up the front of its entrance. The church was in need of repair, as were most of the buildings in Port Gaynor, but as the church was still dry inside, the diocese would not cover the costs of renovation. This place was thought a haven for anyone who believed in any god they chose to believe in. This particular church —though Catholic in denomination—welcomed all, and taught from all the holy books in a way to include as many of the diverse faithful residents as possible. This forward-thinking ethos was led by the church's pastor, Jacoby Martin. With St Jude's being the only holy building of any faith in the area —aside from the now dilapidated and abandoned Old Chapel which stood like a monolith on the edge of the cliffs—and with the port attracting many workers from all over, having a multi-faith church service made sense... At least it did to Jacoby. Though he knew that if his archbishop or any holy elders heard about what he was doing, he would be censured. But Jacoby felt that his god would want this. Barely a priest for 5 years, and just reaching his late-twenties, he believed that he brought a fresh set of beliefs to the table, one not hampered by the dogma carried by the elder clergy who still reveled in fire and brimstone with an exclusionary hatred. Besides, the town was small, and if only the Catholics came to service, the church would barely be a sixth full. At least his way, he had many faces to speak his universal message of hope to.

Jacoby was dressed in jeans and an oversized knitted jumper as he snuffed out the candles on either side of the church's altar. With a feeling of dejection, he glanced over his shoulder at the rows of empty pews behind him. The harsh weather had kept people away from St Jude's for yet another day, leading to yet another canceled service.

"Maybe tomorrow," Jacoby mumbled to himself. "Maybe tomorrow."

With the last candle extinguished, he raised his voice to be heard at the back of the pews, "I'll keep the heating on. You can let yourself out in the morning!"

A grumbled moan from a rear pew could be heard from an unseen man.

"Good night!" Jacoby followed with a smile, as he walked over to a side door, and went through to the small rectory. In reality, that was just a fancy word for a small apartment attached to the church building. A kitchenette, bedroom, and living room combo, leading to a small bathroom at the far end. Hardly worthy of a moniker like 'rectory', but all that Jacoby needed. He had felt bad that the local drunk regularly felt the need to sleep in the church instead of his own house. One Jacoby knew for a fact that the man had. But he didn't mind. It was just that the pews were far from comfortable. The man had been offered more pillows and blankets on multiple occasions, which were all denied. All he wanted and ever took was a single blanket. Jacoby was not one to say no, though. After all, St Jude's was a refuge as well as a house of worship. This became the routine on most nights. The ones where the man wasn't snoring in a stupor at the back of the church were those where the alcohol would have dragged him into unconsciousness before he could make it to this holy sanctuary. It was only those nights where the man had enough of his faculties, where he would be able to make it to his back pew to fall into an unconscious slumber.

A loud bang of the church doors swinging open woke Pastor Jacoby up from what was a lovely dream. One where he could pretend he was not a Catholic priest and could live out his debauched fantasies with Bella Mercer, the woman of his dreams—the woman who also ran the bakery on the other side of the town. Though he loved his faith, he sometimes wished he was a priest within a more nonconformist denomination, one where he didn't have to take vows of celibacy. *But needs must whilst the devil lurks*, as his grandmother used to tell him. So, Jacoby would remain content to live out his libido in the dreamscapes of his subconscious, all for the greater good.

Slowly moving out of his bed, he grabbed the dressing gown that draped over the bedpost, then clumsily put it on.

Walking from the rectory into the church, the wind blew its forceful gusts in a mindless rage into the church through its now wide-open doors, echoing throughout the stone building.

Jacoby grumbled, and he walked down the

nave. His bare feet stung as they touched the icy chill of the large stone slabs below.

As he passed the back pews, Jacoby noticed that 'Mike the Drunk' (as the town not so lovingly referred to him) was no longer snoring away, but was nowhere to be seen. All that was left was the single blanket that Jacoby had left out for him.

"You weren't born in a barn, Mike," Jacoby muttered as he pushed the large wooden doors to close, an action that was very difficult against the gale that now blew violently inward, carrying with it rain and debris picked up in the storm.

He hoped that the drunk man would not be stupid and would find his way safely back to his own house, instead of in a ditch somewhere. He had lost count of the times that he had a call from the police about finding Mike almost hypothermic in the dirt somewhere, or in a shop doorway. Not that Jacoby minded the call, as his job was to be the shepherd of the community. Mike the Drunk, though, was somewhat of a lost cause. Jacoby knew it was only a matter of time before that man's body would give up to the poison he drank by the bottle, but Jacoby would nevertheless still provide shelter if he could, and would pick Mike up when he was found passed out somewhere. Mike was always silent in his thanks, but never argued or fought. He just nodded and did what he was told. The only thing he ever spoke out against was when Jacoby tried to talk to him about his god.

"God don't want me," the drunk had mumbled

on many occasions. So, if Jacoby couldn't save the man's soul, he would at least try to help his body.

The increasing battering rain felt like razors against Michael's face as he ran down the empty midnight street in a flood of panicked tears. He did not care that the ice storm was now at its zenith and that the town was enduring the worst punishment it had done for the past few days. He was too drunk to feel much of the cold being forced upon him, but his fear was not out of inebriation.

His anguished cries were muffled by the wind as he staggered further onward.

Deep in his stupor on the back pew of St Jude's, Mike the Drunk's dreams reeled with forgotten nightmares, and his past attacked him with images of the events that led to the ruin of his life.

Alcohol may have been slowly killing him, but it was all he could do to stop those horrific visions enveloping him in his hours of consciousness. Normally, that liquid would cause his dreams to be vacant and blank. But sometimes, just sometimes, the veil of sleep would not be dulled by his alcohol intake. Sometimes, a clarity would force its way through the drunken haze and show Michael's dreaming eyes the horrific memories that he so feared—just as it had tonight. Yet tonight was also slightly different from the others. Tonight he woke up in the pews to the sound of a laugh of a girl from his past. A laugh that carried on as he sat up and looked around the church pews. A laugh that traversed his dreams and followed him back into reality. A laugh he still heard as he ran down the stormy roads.

This man, Mike the Drunk, legally known as Michael Nádasdy, broke into sobs as this cackling laugh got even louder, despite how far he went.

He screamed in torment as he ran through the icy rain. The laugh still continued in his ears, and as it did, his memories swam with visions of *that* house. *That* girl. Visions of the gun he had held. Visions of the people he had murdered.

His eyesight was not only blurred by the tears in his eyes, or by the alcohol still in his blood, but the storm had become a blanket of murkiness that hampered any clear path ahead. The rain was like a curtain for all in front of him. It was only when his scrambling feet hit the pebbles that he knew full well where he was, that he was on the town's thin pebble beach, and that the vast expanse of the Pacific Ocean lay just in front of him.

As he staggered closer, the sound of the tumultuous waves crashing against the port, almost eclipsing the storm's raging howls and the wailing laughter within his mind.

As his feet hit the water line, Michael collapsed with exhaustion to his knees, into the shallow water. The waterlogged pebbles collided with his kneecaps, stinging as they hit, but that pain was a distant thought to what his mind was now going through.

He continued to scream as his sobering clarity focused his mind on the events that happened many years ago. The time he first heard that child's laugh. That child sat on the altar mocking him. That eyeless child and the demon squatting within her soul.

"Where are you?" Those words were a ghostly refrain that carried on the stormy wind toward Michael, causing his cries to subside from shock almost immediately. He quickly and fearfully glanced around in a panic, trying to focus on anything through the pervasive rain. But he could not see anyone around him.

He also noticed that the laughter had stopped.

"Father Michael!" the horrific voice called again, from far away. That young girl's voice was twisted by evil that echoed in his dreams over the years since that night.

"*Faaaathheerrr Micchhhaaaeeell!*"

This time, it was not a distant, ghostly voice. It was clearer. It was present and coming from near to him. Not from the shore, but from somewhere in the ocean ahead.

Didn't it?

He tried to focus.

It wasn't in his mind... *Something* was here. That thing was here.

Then... nothing.

Nothing but the wind and the rain and the sounds of his own sobbing.

His thoughts spiraled. It must have been his mind. A drunkard's imagination running rampant, surely.

He collapsed further down onto the pebbles, in a heap, as the waves crashed around him.

"I'm sorry," he blubbed, apologizing to no one but himself. An apology to his soul, for all the evil he had scarred upon it.

The waves continued to crash into him, diminutive versions of the monstrous ones that raged only a short distance ahead of him.

As was usual at this stage of his inebriation, his mind traversed beyond guilt and to the stage of planned renewal. He was being stupid, he thought to himself. Being out here was doing nothing for anyone. Punishing himself was all well and good—and had been something he was now an expert at—but amends could only be offered in the service of others. These types of thoughts would usually remain until the next drop of liquor passed his lips, and the whole cycle would restart. But then, just as he was making promises to himself, that voice pulled him out of it with a jolt...

"*There you are!*" That voice again, this time clearer, and the laughing cackle then continued.

Michael looked up, and ahead of him, upon the crest of a large wave, a small boat came into view. A small wooden boat, with a faint lamp at its bow, guiding the way.

"I *finally* found you!"

Michael wiped his eyes and felt his stomach twist as the impossible figures within the boat became clearer.

Traversing over the top of the wave, passing about twenty feet in front of him, two skeletal figures frantically tried to paddle the boat, as another figure between them leaned over the side, calling out to Michael.

"It can't be," Michael sobbed, staring ahead. The waves continued to hit his collapsed frame in force, getting bigger and angrier with each subsequent round. But he could only stare ahead in terror.

"I'm free, priest!" The young, eyeless girl shouted. "And I have *found* you! After years of darkness, I have found you." The glee was so evident in her voice that the storm could not mask it. She leaned over the side of the boat toward the shore, toward Michael, and emitted her sickening laugh louder than ever. Her large eyeless sockets, wide and bloody, stared deeply toward him.

At that exact moment, the water swelled violently as an almighty wave started building toward shore. Toward Michael.

Jacoby's morning ritual consisted of two staple things; coffee, followed by a second cup. He was a man of his god, yet not a man of morning. Ever since childhood, his body could barely adapt to being awake before lunchtime. Luckily for him, with Port Gaynor being a town where nothing really happened before 11am, and with all services at St Jude's being evening ones, his desire to sleep was a gift that he normally appreciated every morning.

But not today.

Today he was woken up by a constant banging. The second time during his sleep, that noise from the church had awoken him.

Through a half-asleep daze, Jacoby finished putting his priest's garb on and lazily walked out of the rectory and into the church. The banging at the door remained constant.

Opening the large wooden door, a woman in her late sixties, dressed in a black suit, with her white hair pulled back over her pointed features, stood facing him as the storm swirled in the town behind her.

"Uh hello?" Jacoby said as a question.

The woman glanced down at the door handle and then back up at the priest. "You don't lock your doors?" she asked, with a thick accent that was unfamiliar to him.

"No," he replied. "It's a small town and anyone's welcome. Anyway, what are they going to steal? A candle?" Her expression remained blank to his jocular tone. "Anyway," he continued. "I'm Jacoby Martin. Pastor at St Jude's. How can I help?"

"May I enter?" she asked. "It is not very hospitable out here."

"Oh, I-I'm sorry," he stuttered, standing back from the doorway to let her in. "Please, come in."

"So, what brings you here?" Jacoby asked softly, as he closed the door behind her. "I've not seen you around here before."

"My name is Sarah Babbidge." Her words were cold, devoid of emotion, and carried a tone of impatience. "I'm an administrator from St Peter's Basilica."

"The Vatican?" Jacoby almost coughed in surprise. "What are you doing at St Jude's?"

"I need you to assist." Sarah's expression gave as little information as her words.

"Is this about my position here?" Jacoby couldn't help but feel that this woman's presence was not a good thing. Maybe she was here because of how he didn't just speak from the bible in his services. Did they find out? Did someone complain?

"No, this is not about you."

"If you don't mind me asking, what are you an administrator of?"

Sarah Babbidge smiled an impatient smile, as she replied blankly, with one single, yet terrifying word.

"Demons."

Two

As Michael came to, he could no longer hear the sounds of the storm, no longer feel the sharp pebbles underneath his body. Instead, he felt only warm grass beneath him. He felt the glowing midday sun upon his skin. He felt far, far away from that wave that had risen ahead of him, then swept him out to the sea in a matter of seconds.

Opening his eyes, he felt no pain, he only felt a calm. A large expanse of green fields stretched around him as far as he could see, split up with occasional groves of trees.

"To think," the now all-too-familiar voice said. "The land we are on will one day become one of perversion and idolatry. One beholden to the lies you will build to your sky-god."

Michael's jaw dropped as he saw Petra standing there. Still eyeless. Still bloody. Still, exactly as she had been in that stone chamber. Smiling at him.

"Y-you can't be here," Michael managed to weakly say.

"I can't be in your dreams?" Petra laughed. Her voice was free of the demonic twang it had before. She now sounded as she would have done before the horrors entered her life. Yet her eyes were still gouged out, her body was still covered in bites and lacerations, and her petticoat was still drenched in fresh blood.

Michael glanced around him. None of this felt like a dream, though there was no way he could actually be standing in this idyllic landscape.

"You are now in a field in Italy, before it was called that, of course." Petra smiled as she opened her arms to motion to all the surroundings. "We are standing on the very site where your holiest of churches will one day be built."

Michael started to feel woozy. "I–" was all he managed to say before his whole stomach wretched and a torrent of seawater ejected itself from his insides.

Petra ignored his actions and pointed downward to the ground. Her voice began to lose its innocent lilt, and a deep guttural edge began to tinge her accent. "Beneath here, before the bastard Symmachus had his temple of filth erected, he ordered a prison to be built deep below. A prison where the heralds of the seas will be kept. Where your perverse brethren took us and tortured us. Where your whore-god allowed us to be kept in torment, as other gods slumbered."

Reeling from his whole body feeling waves of intense nausea, Michael could not fully comprehend what was being said. "*Pope* Symmachus?" he managed to ask.

"That walking abortion created what he lovingly referred to as abyssus damnatio." Her smile faltered as she slowly approached Michael. Her hollow, bloody sockets seemed to stare directly at him. Her words became more twisted and hate-filled with each word she uttered. "A hell for us, built below. A hell for what he saw as hellish. A hell where we were forced to endure your order's deepest perversions, over and over... All in the name of your whore-god. Why did you dream us here?"

She moved even closer.

Michael began to smell an encroaching aroma of rotten fish. But it was not from Petra. He began to smell it on his own body. Barely grasping onto consciousness, and trying to focus on what the demon child was saying, he started to waver. "What? I didn't, did I?" he managed to ask, weakly.

Petra took another step toward him, "you brought me here and for what? To prove my point? I told you many years ago... I want to show you how wrong you all are." Her words trailed off as she smiled. "Your kind hunted us and kept us in a prison, deep below your holy vomitorium... You forced us to live under your lies... Then I was summoned, and you tried to kill me with your god. Then... nothing. And now we find ourselves here? For what purpose? Have you given up?"

Michael's eyes fluttered as he still tried to focus, but his stomach began to twist again, and his mind became cloudier. He wanted to ask what she was talking about.

Suddenly, an arm appeared from behind Michael and grasped him by the shoulder of his jumper. As the arm pulled and wrenched him upward, seawater exploded from all around. The Italian landscape, as well as the eyeless girl, was suddenly ripped away as Michael's body was lifted up...

...and out of the tumultuous storm-riddled sea, half a mile out from where the dock of Port Gaynor lay.

As Michael began to lose consciousness, he could only see the battering rain and the surrounding darkness around him.

"Keep breathing..." he heard someone in the far distance shout at him.

Then... darkness. Only darkness

Anna Ólafsdóttir kicked the bottom of the door open with her snow boot, dislodging it from the ill-fitting frame's grasp. A ritual she had repeated every time she entered here. To her, this wasn't a problem that needed fixing, but just something that had to be done to get the door open. An added security measure to the ramshackle port office.

This office was small, creaky, and hardly safe

from the elements. With the thin gaps at the edges of the window frames, it let the wind in, but like the church nearby, it still did its job despite the state it was in.

After all, Anna had warm clothes and a heater. The toilet in the back of the office flushed, and the radio still worked. Nothing else was needed. And this was just how she liked life, with what was needed. No more, no less. Being in her early thirties, she was often accused of wasting her life in this town, in this job, but she never felt that. This town was her home, for better or worse.

The one thing she did not like was having to come into the port office in the middle of a storm. In this weather, no boats should ever be out on the seas. She and all the fishermen should be in their homes, wrapped up warm. She had already witnessed the devastation that greed had wrought when fishing trawlers ignored common sense and placed money into the same pot as their stupidity. Sure, during a storm, you could catch more fish due to the large swells in the sea, making the sea life below more active. But *'Could' and 'Should' are not the same thing*, as the big sign above her boldly stated on etched wood.

And here she was *again*, having to try to call a trawler back from danger. One ship that had almost consistently flouted the rules during each storm that hit Port Gaynor, and one that refused to listen to her authority.

With the storm clouds making 11am look like

11pm, Anna did not have a good feeling about what may happen to the ship called the *Annabel Lee*.

She had just sat down in front of a fire, with a cup of tea and a book, when Emmet Jones called her at home. From his lighthouse on the cliffs, Emmet could see the distinctive blue and red lights of the *Annabelle Lee* out by Hinkley Bay—Out where the mackerel shoals would be active.

Anna took a deep breath as she picked up the radio mic, clicking the button on the side. "Annabelle Lee, Annabelle Lee," she said loudly and clearly into it. "This is Port Gaynor calling the vessel Annabelle Lee. Come in, over."

She waited for a few moments.

Nothing but static.

Shaking her head, she clicked the button again and spoke. "Annabelle Lee, this is Port Gaynor, Come in." Her exasperation started to get the best of her. "Dad, pick up the goddamn fucking radio!"

The radio sharply cracked as a voice came over it, shouting to be heard over the sounds of the storm winds alongside it. "Baby girl, I was about to call in!" the deep male voice shouted, sounding very far away. "We're coming back."

"Good! Hurry the hell up!" Anna's anger started to build due to her father's carefree tone. "You shouldn't be out there. I told you—"

"I found someone in the water," her father shouted, cutting her complaint off. "That bum who's always drunk outside the bar."

Anna couldn't find any words to reply. She just stared ahead, out of the window, at the stormy seas ahead.

"He was face down in the blue," her father continued. "He nearly got caught in the nets." Behind his shouted words, the storm sounded terrifyingly violent, with banshee-like wails and drumming rain, all of it amplified over the radio, as well as the sound of the battering storm upon the port office.

"Stupid drunk," Anna mumbled as she shook her head and replied into the mic, "You see, *this* is what happens when you go out in a storm. It can kill you!"

"No, baby girl," her father shouted. "I don't know how it happened, but the man's alive. Swallowed lots of water, but... He's breathing. Somehow."

As Ólaf Hansson, the captain of the *Annabelle Lee*, father to the port master, stepped off his boat and onto the wooden jetty at Port Gaynor dock, he felt a bit sick. He always did when he stepped off from the water and onto land. Despite his immense stature, the land always had made him feel weak. He only ever felt well on the seas, and no one, not even his own daughter, could stop him from going out when he felt the call. He knew going out in the storm was a gamble, but if the water took him, so be it. It was how he wanted to go, after all. And if he came back, he would make money with the catch of fish, hopefully enough to maintain his precious *Annabelle Lee* and pay for the next trip's provisions—not to mention the fine that his daughter would levy upon him for breaking the rules.

Today, though, was a big disappointment for him. *Annabelle Lee*'s fishing ended after only a few hours when he found the floating body of Mike the Drunk. He only had a chance to get a small haul of mackerel in when his body floated by.

"Ólaf!" came the disappointed shout from the end of the jetty, as Anna stood outside her port office, looking angrily at her father on his boat. The heavy cold rain doing nothing to dull the severity of her tone.

He could feel her annoyance despite the actual storm between them, and she only ever called him by his name when she was angry with him, which was almost all the time. Since they had arrived in the United States, when he and his then four-year-old daughter left their native Iceland, he had tried his best to raise her as well as he could. But all he knew was how to trawl the seas, and that meant he was absent for large swathes of her childhood. Instead of raising her himself, various members of the town did so instead. An ever-changing procession of people willing to look after her whilst he went off in search of fish. He could not blame anyone but himself, that the days of her calling him 'pabbi' were extinct. Maybe she would call him that on his birthday, maybe when she needed something, but their relationship was not what he wanted it to be, and he knew that it was all his fault.

Turning to the *Annabelle Lee*, Ólaf leaned down over the side of his boat and picked up the unconscious body of Michael Nádasdy. In the Icelandic's gigantic arms, Michael looked like a small boy in a giant's hold.

As Ólaf approached the port office where Anna stood, he weakly smiled at her in apology.

"You went out alone again?" Anna said in disappointment as she shook her head. "How stupid are you?"

"Not now, Anna." Ólaf said, motioning to the unconscious man in his arms. "Where's the doctor?"

"The Old Chapel?" Jacoby asked in confusion. "Why, in god's name, do you want to go there? It's derelict. And also it's totally unsafe. It's been condemned by the county for the past decade."

Above them, as she spoke, thunder crashed loudly. Cutting off Jacoby's questioning. The storm outside was getting more and more violent with each passing moment.

"You hear that?" Sarah spoke softly and then motioned above her. "You understand that this is not a normal storm, don't you? It's a portent. It is a warning of what's coming here. Even nature screams when it fears demise. It sees all. And time is not on our side. Evil is on the move."

Jacoby could only stare at her. He hated the fire and brimstone teachings that the older generations of priests based their faiths on. And hearing this strange woman speaking like that made him want to throw her out of St Jude's. But he had no choice. He had to go with her to the Old Chapel. He just wouldn't be happy about it.

Naked, emaciated, and bloodied, a woman walked slowly through a verdant forest. Each step this young woman took left a blot on the grass beneath her. A dark shadow that sucked all the life out of the surrounding greenery. Each step she took was a nail in the coffin of all that lived in its passing presence.

This figure's hair was long and unkempt. Its eyes were healed sockets, and she still turned to look as if they could see. Her body was a mass of torment. Every inch of her skin had a burned symbol scarred into it. Her whole being was a testament to an incredible amount of pain and torment.

THREE

The thick fog that had clouded Michael's dreams began to dissipate. As his consciousness crawled back from the brink, his eyes opened, his lids heavy. The pale ceiling of the hospital room soon came into focus, and a deep confusion swelled from within him. Memories of the sea, the boat with skeletons, that demonic girl, and then the green Italian fields, were now just vague imprints on his hungover mind. He felt like he always did when waking up from a heavy night, but now his lungs and bones felt on fire.

"He's awake," a male voice said.

"Mr.... Nada-na," a female voice stuttered in pronunciation.

"Nah-dojsh-dee," the doctor corrected.

Michael was still partially within his dreaming mind, battered by the vast amount of alcohol in his blood, as well as seawater in his lungs.

"Michael, you're in the hospital. My name is

Doctor Huw Atkins. Do you remember me? I treated you a few years ago?"

Michael, slowly getting his focus, nodded to the doctor. "Why am I here?" he weakly asked.

"Why?" the doctor smiled. "Well, we can't just let you die, can we?"

Michael winced as the soreness in his lungs throbbed.

"You should start to feel better over the next few weeks, as long as you take the medicine we're prescribing and stay off the booze," Doctor Atkins continued. "If you don't, I can tell you plainly that your body will not recover. It is imperative you stay here and do all we say, okay? You should have died out there, but you were damn lucky you didn't. Any longer living like you did, you would have died anyway from the alcohol."

"Doctor?" the female voice said worriedly. "Tox just came back."

"Will I be surprised?" the doctor asked.

Michael lifted his heavy head and saw the young nurse, Agnes Stahl, reading from a chart.

"0.4.," she said, with shock in her voice.

"Well," the doctor turned to Michael wide-eyed. "I think that may be the only reason the sea didn't kill you. The bad news is, we have to manage your addiction. The withdrawals will do a lot of damage in your present state if not monitored and medicated correctly." He turned to Agnes. "We need to start a dopamine course."

The words, though, drifted away as Michael's

hazy gaze refocused beyond the nurse, in to the corner of the room, to what stood behind the open room door.

Standing there, silently, peering out at him with one of her bloodied, empty eye sockets, was Petra. Complete with her demonic smile, she stared emptily in his direction. Dressed still in her bloodied nightie, she looked just as she was that night, just as she did on the boat, and just as she did in the fields in his mind.

"No..." Michael moaned as he started to writhe in his bed. "You can't be here!"

Doctor Atkins and Agnes, alarmed by this sudden outburst, ran up to Michael's bedside. Restraining him, they tried their best to stop this patient from ripping out his IV, or causing himself any more harm than he already had done.

"Get away from me!" Michael screamed at the apparition, as his strength returned quickly, bolstered by his sheer panic.

Agnes, realizing that he was staring past them with a terrified expression, turned to see what was causing his fear and such a violent reaction. But when she turned, there was nothing to be seen. Just a wall and an open door.

"You're not here, demon!" Michael continued. "I saw you die!"

"He's hallucinating," Agnes said, as Doctor Atkins held down Michael's shoulders.

"Administer 5 mg of haloperidol," he said to Agnes as his gaze dropped down to Michael.

"Please calm down. There's nothing there. It is all in your mind."

But Michael could only stare at the vision of the monstrous Petra, still in the corner of the hospital room, half behind the door, waving silently at him with a sickeningly gleeful grin on her bloodied and wounded face. From every orifice on her broken body, a black smoke trickled out. From her eye sockets, nose, mouth and ears, this almost liquid looking smoke trailed upwards.

This smoke flitted around the room and curled up the bodies of the doctor and nurse. They unwittingly breathed it deep inside.

The rain slashed down, driven by the incessant winds, as Sarah and Jacoby approached the broken remains of the Old Chapel on the cliffs of Port Gaynor. Its dilapidated form was almost swallowed by the darkness and the circling storm around it. At the far end of the building, the high cliffs it was built on stretched out into eternal blackness, with over a hundred foot drop to jagged rocks below. Like a huge void in the night, the storm masked any sea vista these cliffs looked out toward.

At the large wooden entrance recessed in a stone archway, Jacoby pulled out a large key from his drenched coat and jammed it onto the lock as quickly as he could. Not that he needed a key. Anyone could break down this door with the minimum of effort. Though anxious to escape the storm, he hurried as he twisted the key.

Inside the abandoned chapel, the air was thick and moist. The rain had broken through some of the smashed windows and fallen down onto the rotten pews below.

The door finally unlocked and swung inward. Jacoby, with an exasperated grunt, entered first. Sarah followed him, looking around like a hawk. With a flashlight in her hand, she shone it all around the chapel, her eyes following the beam as it went, tracing the environment as she searched for something specific.

Slamming the large door behind them did little to quell the howl of the winds, which broke into the building from a large hole in the roof.

"What are we here for?" Jacoby asked, expecting no real answer. "What has this chapel to do with anything? Does the diocese want to restore it?"

Sarah, with her gaze not relenting from scanning the church with her light, answered almost on autopilot. "we are looking for a hidden entrance."

"Hidden?" He sighed as he felt that he was being taken for a fool. "Do you really need me here?"

"I haven't got time to boil down over a thousand years of discovery and ancient metaphysical texts into a tasty soundbite that you can fathom..." Sarah took a breath and tried to compose her thoughts. The headache she had had since leaving Italy was pounding. A handful of painkillers had done nothing to quell the stabbing feeling inside her brain.

Without giving him a chance to reply, she continued. "Suffice to say, that you are a holy figure. I need holiness. You are a key. And this Old Chapel has what we need, hopefully."

"You're not holy? You're from the Vatican. Aren't you ordained?"

Bursting out with a loud guffaw, Sarah shook her head, finding the notion hilarious yet still preposterous. "Ordained? Me?"

"So, who are you in all this?"

"I do what needs to be done." Sarah's smile faltered as she spoke. "Whatever the church needs."

"What does that mean?"

"I'm the instrument needed when you turn a blind eye." Looking at his blank expression, she smirked. "I don't expect you to understand, suffice to say I look after things that do not exist, should not exist."

"And here? What's this place got to do with it?"

Rolling her eyes, Sarah composed herself for a moment, realizing she had to explain herself more if she was going to be able to carry on. "I will tell you this, but I need you to just listen and not argue. Okay?"

He just stared back, unsure of anything he could say that would help.

"I can say that there is an evil coming to this

town. It's coming because it was birthed here."

"You're being quite vague."

"We are dealing with a mess of metaphor and code, truth hidden behind half shadow and lies from scrolls thousands of years old. Until now, no one put two and two together what the significance of this town was, or that it would be about somewhere in the fucking United States, of all places! Years before it even existed as a town. But when that *thing* spoke... It made a lot of old texts clearer. Get it?"

"Not really. What thing? What are you talking about?"

"This chapel was not always the building of your god. We have to look below."

"My god?" Jacoby had more or less confirmed his feeling that this woman was not sane, and most likely not who she said she was.

"The devil is a god to some, you know?"

"You're saying this is a satanic place?" Jacoby knew he was playing into this delusion, but he had to know what she was believing was happening, so he could better get her the help she needed.

"Satanist, Luciferian, Occultist... One of them, I presume," Sarah returned to scanning the ruined church with her flashlight. The beam danced over the cracked walls. Faded frescoes depicted scenes of saints and sinners passed before her torch light, but she paid them little attention. Her focus was on the worn stones themselves. One by one, looking for a clue. Looking for anything.

"Where is it?" she muttered. "It has to be here."

The naked and bloodied Petra staggered along the hot streets, her feet a mass of fresh wounds from the journey walked so far. Hundreds of miles across the field, stone and mud. But she did not mind the pain; she could not even feel it. She did not think about it. She did not think of *anything*. For Petra was essentially dead. All that was left of her was a body and the thing within her. The thing that drove her. The thing that walked from her prison beneath the holy capital. And from her body, the black smoke still erupted, reaching out and coating all around her.

Her eyeless sockets stared ahead, with each step she took being slow and labored. The sun beat down on her leathery, pale skin, reflecting off the glass-fronted buildings that lined this city street. The heat that beat down was intense, and the asphalt beneath her reflected that heat back up in a haze, not that she knew. She just knew the journey she was taking.

"Mon Dieu!" a concerned old man exclaimed, as he walked on the sidewalk toward her. This was one more person who had sealed their own fate by being in the wrong place at the wrong time.

The old man, though, was not focused on her. His shock was directed toward the mass of people that walked behind her. A grotesque sight of dozens upon dozens of people, staggering after this naked figure. The people all had the same expressions of vacancy, of having nothing inside them bar a strange sort of psychosis.

Before the shocked old man could get away, as Petra walked closer, his eye twitched as something affected him. Suddenly, a sharp pain rang through his ears, and he fell to his knees onto the sidewalk with a painful crack. But the pain shooting through his mind was what made him scream, not his hip breaking from his fall. He screamed for a few moments, then fell quickly silent.

Within a few seconds, the screams turned into a light giggle as the old man looked up at the sky. His eyes were wide. His grin, terrifying. Whatever this old man's name used to be, it was now lost to him. Whatever he used to think was now lost to him. For he was no longer himself.

Staggering to his feet, he smiled the same terrifying smile as all those that followed Petra and started to walk along at the same pace, joining this infernal parade.

Petra staggered on by not looking at what was happening around her. She had no eyes, nor inclination to look, and didn't need to. She only wished to walk on.

In the city around her, hundreds of screams could also be heard. In buildings, on adjacent streets, and everywhere else. Screams like that of the old man, ones that also did not last long, and ones that turned into a horrifying giggle. Soon, the procession grew larger and larger as each new acolyte was converted and joined the ranks in line. Like grinning zombies of a dark, religious obsession, they followed without question, without sanity, without even a thought.

Petra may have only entered the city a short time ago, but by the time she and her horde would reach the shoreline less than a mile ahead, there would be few sane, or living people here left.

Ólaf Hansson's head was pounding. He had sat on the corner of his metal-framed bed for the past hour, rubbing his thick fingers on his temples, trying to quell the pain somehow. The pills he swallowed hours ago had done nothing to lessen the sharp agony he was now being subjected to.

From the moment he pulled that man out of the ocean, this pain had sat in his head. A pain that only seemed to get worse by the moment. He was used to hangovers as well as migraines, and never let that pain slow him down. It was just pain, after all. This though. This was different. This was debilitating. This was somehow unnatural.

His thoughts drifted back to the drunk man. A man Ólaf knew over the years. A man who Ólaf thought did not deserve to be saved. But death was not Ólaf's to allow. So despite having a bad opinion of the man, Ólaf had to save him.

The single bare lightbulb hanging in the center

of his room shone a murky yellow glow, yet to Ólaf, it still seemed too bright. It felt blinding in its luminescence.

The bed's frame creaked as he stood up clumsily from it. He then staggered over to the far side of the room, then flicked the light switch to off, casting him into immediate and almost total darkness. A darkness that only lessened the pain by a tiny fraction. But the pain in his head still pounded, worse and worse, with each heartbeat. Suddenly, his worst thoughts began to spin and collide, twisting his reality as they crept out of the depths of his subconscious.

Deep in the cocoon of his medicated slumber, Michael found a fleeting solace. The sedation had plunged him into a realm of oblivion, a respite from the haunting visions that had clung to him like shadows. In the silence of this chemically induced sleep, Michael's mind was a blank canvas, devoid of any dreams and, more importantly, free from that thing. That impossible thing.

The years had etched lines of weariness onto Michael's face, a testament to the toll exacted by time and the weight of guilt that had settled upon his shoulders since that fateful night in 1975. And before this night, those memories were the things that only haunted his sleeping mind. Yet earlier they had turned from dark specters and seemed to walk into the light and face him head-on in his own waking world. His memories had seemingly manifested, and they were angry at what he had done, mocking him with a shocking malevolence. But within the embrace of the sedative's grip, he temporarily escaped these clutches, finding a vacant reprieve.

Yet, unbeknownst to the unconscious Michael, that malevolent force stirred within the recesses of his mind. That evil, deep in the darkness, had taken root in his psyche, lying dormant yet patient.

The hospital room, as tranquil as it was, and as blank as Michael's dreams were, unwittingly concealed the brewing tempest held in his mind that begged to get out.

Petra's hollow sockets gleamed with perverse satisfaction as she took the first step into the shallow waters of the city's bay side. The smoke from her still shooting out.

The sun above still rained down its intense heat, highlighting the ghastly scene that now unfolded in the shocking clarity of the summer's day.

Without any hesitation, the evil pressed forward, walking deeper and deeper into the waters that stretched out eternally before her.

The waves, with a serene calm, wrapped around

her figure, like serpentine tendrils eager to embrace their new malevolent guest.

As Petra descended further into the shallows, the waters obediently licked at her bony frame. The smoke from her also descended. Not extinguished by the water, but became one with it, darkening the sea it touched.

Her ghastly smile persisted as Petra advanced, the waterline rising with each passing moment, swallowing her in its cold, brackish depths. The city behind echoed with the shuffling footsteps of her acolytes, the surreal procession following their demonic leader into the watery abyss. Their minds were too busily entangled in her malevolent web of influence, which forced them to follow blindly, not knowing the dangers ahead.

Neck-deep, paying no heed to the trailing masses behind her, Petra descended beneath the water with otherworldly grace, continuing to walk further and further out. Her followers, however, were not as fortunate. This cursed throng attempted to mimic their leader by walking out into the blue.

One by one, the parade contorted beneath the surface, their limbs entangled in a dance of agony. Their expression morphed into silent screams as saltwater invaded their lungs. And one by one, their bodies ascended to the surface like ghostly apparitions, lifeless. Betrayed by the one they followed.

The bay, once a haven for fun-seeking tourists,

had transformed into a nightmarish tableau. Hundreds of waterlogged corpses, men, women, and children, floated in a grotesque ballet, an aquatic graveyard at the edge of this once happy city. Yet, the remnants of the cursed procession persisted. Those still on the shore, with their minds ensnared by Petra's demonic aura, clambered over the fallen bodies of their brethren in a macabre climb toward their own inevitable fate.

More horror soon folded as the next wave of followers stepped into the seas, uncaring of the tragedy befalling their predecessors. These desperate figures moved with an unsettling determination, finding the openings among the already floating dead, stepping into the cold embrace of the sea to meet their own end. And not one of them cared. They only knew the madness that Petra gifted them. Their leader. Their god. Their executioner.

As the cursed parade continued, the lack of noise from this mass extinction was all the more terrifying. Only the sound of their bodies walking into the water and the occasional thrashing could be heard. No screams. No cries. No whimpers. The shoreline had become a surreal stage, where the drama of suicidal madness played out in a haunting repetition. Each person, lost to the depths, added to the grotesquery of the unholy curse that Petra had unleashed upon the city.

Four

As Michael's eyes lazily fluttered open, and the darkness of his sedation wore off, he tried to piece together where he was. He was used to waking up in strange places, with a pounding hangover, so felt no panic as the white walls and room became clearer.

Then the vague memories of what had happened before came back. The sea. The child. The fields. The doctor. The—

"Ah, there you are!"

That voice. That *evil* voice.

Scrambling his thoughts into focus, Michael looked around the room in a panic, desperate to see where she was. His returned tormenter.

"I can finally talk, finally exist. No longer a shadow in my would-be murderer's mind."

Michael tried to focus, but his body ached, his head ached, everything ached. The damage he had sustained from the sea was beyond substantial; he had fractured ribs and bruises over most of his body. So, trying to stand up and run was too much for him to bear. He could only panic as a cold chill swept over him. He then glanced at the door, hoping to see a doctor passing, but it was closed.

He then tried to scream for help, but what came out was a hoarse croak. The seawater that flooded his lungs had left some damage as his whole chest felt on fire. He could only speak in a quiet croak

"Please," came the whimper from his throat. "You can't be real."

At the foot of his hospital bed, appearing like a giant spider, crawling over the metal end rail, the small demonic Petra appeared. Moving in a jolting, unnatural motion, she didn't look a minute older than she was on that night long ago.

"Oh I am real, priest," the sinister child said, now perched on the end rail, as she stared at him with her empty, bloody sockets.

For the first time, her long hair fell to one side, exposing the top of her forehead, which now had a small black hole in it. A bullet hole. A hole that dripped fresh blood.

"Please," he tried to say again.

"You can hear me. You can see me. Is that not real?" She started to crawl off of the rail and up the bed, not once taking her empty stare off of him.

"And now, unlike those many years ago, I am not chained." She got closer to him, her crawl slow and terrifying.

Tears fell from Michael's eyes as he shut them, trying to blot out the monster crawling above him.

Unable to stay in the dark, Michael slowly opened his eyes and was met with the horrible image of Petra's face, only a few inches from his own, grinning down at him. Blood from her wounds dripped onto him.

Through his damaged vocal cords, Michael managed to scream in a primal terror.

"Witness the beautiful madness," the thing screamed at him.

In the break room, on the ground floor of the hospital, Doctor Atkins sat in pain. He had sent Agnes home as she was feeling ill, and with two other nurses on duty, he knew the night shift would be fine without her. Yet, he refused to take his own advice; being the on-call doctor, there were no others available. His headache had to be managed, and he had to stay on duty.

But the pain he was suffering was intense. A pain that he knew was not usual and was a pain that worried him. Especially as Agnes had said, her headache was intense as well.

His mind swirled as it considered different medical scenarios that could explain both of their current maladies. Was this something they both caught from a patient? A virus that could spread throughout the hospital? He did not know. He could not focus enough on one thing for long.

Then, all of his medical knowledge, all of that wisdom garnered over the sixty-two years he had been on this earth, fell away from him at incredible speed. A primal fear washed over him as he tried to gather his thoughts, but could not think straight. He could not form a sentence in his mind. Something was very wrong. As the pain grew more and more intense, making him feel like a lost child, Doctor Huw Atkins broke down. For over thirty years, this stoic and serious man had been the chief resident at Port Gaynor Hospital. But here and now, in the darkness of the break room, he felt nothing except fear and pain as he wept uncontrollably.

Staggering over to the window, he tried to open it to let in some air. Air that had not been passed through a dirty filter. But as his hand held the latch, his gaze rose and looked outward.

He saw something that made him scream. Something staring back at him. His parents. Long dead. Long violently dead.

Across town, in her small house, Agnes hung dead from a noose she had made with her bedsheets. The pain had become too much. The pills did nothing. The darkness did nothing. Sleep did nothing. Then... as she got more and more desperate, her reality had started to shift.

When she had seen the large mushroom clouds lighting up the sky, soon joined by others in the surrounding distance, her biggest fear had sprung to impossible life, bringing its nuclear hate into only her world. But this was only her vision. This was only in her mind.

Her suicide note read a simple phrase; "God help our souls."

Ólaf Hansson had it no better than Agnes... His heart was breaking as he was failing at being a good father, his biggest fear, failing his kin in the worst possible way.

In the coldness of his cellar, Ólaf was murdering his daughter.

With his large hands wrapped around Anna's throat, he could only watch from deep within his soul, witnessing as his body strangled the life out of her. He had no idea how or why this happened. He did not even remember how he got down here, nor her arriving. He just remembered the pain in his head. Then this.

As Anna's life ebbed away, as her shocked and terrified eyes closed for good, the force that controlled Ólaf to commit such a heinous act was far from finished.

"I need to see you bleed!" he found himself saying.

Without a second's pause, Ólaf then screamed in his mind as he witnessed his hands start to beat and beat and beat upon his daughter's body, with an unrelenting ferocity.

Her skin broke, her bones snapped, and her blood oozed. The more damage he inflicted, the more he found that his body was getting aroused.

Ólaf prayed in his subconscious for his body to stop. Screamed from his mental prison. Screams that had no effect on what he witnessed.

His fears were now manifest, as were Agnes' and Huw's. And as all three breathed, not one saw the trails of black smoke dripping out of them.

An hour later, when Ólaf would come to from the insanity, naked and within the remains of his daughter, he would stagger upstairs, to where he kept his shotgun, and he would without any pause, end his torment with a pull of the trigger.

Little did he know that in the Port Office, Anna was still asleep at her desk. She had not come over that night. She was not in her father's basement. She had no idea what Ólaf Hansson had believed he had done to her. Nor would she ever.

Tears streamed out of Michael's eyes as he stared at the ceiling of his hospital room. He had felt the sadness within Agnes consume her life until the noose snapped her neck. He had felt the abyss of despair that Ólaf had fallen into as he uncontrollably murdered his own daughter in his mind. He had seen through the eyes of his own doctor as he looked out of the window and saw his dead parents.

Ripping the IV from his arm, Michael then tumbled off the side of the bed, falling to the cold linoleum floor.

The laughing in his mind was deafening as he scrambled to his feet, ignoring the girl at the periphery of his vision. No matter where he looked, Petra was there, standing in a corner, out of the window, always staring with her open bloody eyes sockets, always cackling, always tormenting.

He could not witness her torment and torture anymore. He had felt every emotion that her victims had felt, the victims that had touched him. The victims that he had seen Petra stain with her reach.

"I saw that too, priest," Petra gleefully said. "I would like to say I intended to do that, but it seems my effect of being in your reality has its bonuses."

Five

Cardinal Augustine Nivoli lurched down the small steps of the spiral stone staircase that wound below him. This circular brick passageway was lit with small flaming torches on each of its curved sides, casting an archaic hue across the Cardinal's black and red cassock.

Though not an unfit man by any means, being in his seventies made his descent harder each time Augustine had to do it—Not to mention the walk up. One which he was now dreading. But worse than all that was *where* he was going. He dreaded that the most.

One hundred feet above him sat the Vatican archives, in which some of the biggest secrets and artifacts of the faith were held in one of the most secure complexes on earth. Another hundred feet above that, Karol Wojtyła sat signing documents under his assumed name of Pope John Paul II.

Ten minutes later, after descending further and further, Augustine stood, catching his breath in front of a large metal door. This door was fitted with a camera at the top of its large frame, one that pointed down at him.

"Are you going to open up, or am I to stand here all day?" he shouted with a thick Italian accent.

After a few moments, a large clank was heard at the door, as a complex mechanism activated; whirrs and clicks of locking clutches sounded themselves proudly. A louder clank followed as the door opened with a whining creak soon following. Standing on the other side of this door, two guards in priest's garb, each carrying guns, nodded to the Cardinal.

Stepping over the threshold, Augustine smiled at the men as the door closed and locked behind him, emitting a new set of whirrs and clicks from its mechanism.

In this wide corridor ahead of him, the floor, the walls, and the ceiling were all made of stone and adorned with many tiny symbols etched into them. Each of these was a small runic-style symbol, and together they decorated all the surfaces of the corridor in their multiple thousands.

"Where is she?" the Cardinal asked one of the guards.

"In the office, your eminence," the guard said in reverence, with his head bowed.

Nodding, the Cardinal walked onward down the corridor. He felt an ache in the pit of his stomach. The same ache he always felt here.

"It started talking about seven hours ago."

Augustine could only stare at the CCTV monitor in shock as Sarah Babbidge spoke to him.

"We sent someone in, but as you can see," her voice trailed off as she pointed at the monitor.

On the hazy and low-resolution screen, a man in a white lab coat sat facing the wall in a corridor. His shoulders vibrated angrily, as if he was trying to shake off an invisible force.

"What is he doing?" Augustine asked.

Sarah flipped a switch next to the monitor. After a crackle of electricity, the hollow sound from the camera's microphone played out over the small speakers in the security office.

A sinister laugh. Low but malevolent, could be heard and was coming from the man in the lab coat.

"He's been doing that since we called you," Sarah said mournfully.

Augustine turned to her, his expression one of restraint. It would be so easy to panic at times like this, but he was not one to rise to emotion. "And what about the thing?" He asked. "Which one is it?"

Sarah leaned over the keyboard and, after typing in a command, the image on the monitor flicked over to one of a large, dark room. In the center of the room, a naked, eye-less female figure was tied to a metal framed bed. Her hands and arms were shackled, and her body was covered in the same small symbols as were etched into the surfaces of the corridor. Each of the symbols had been burned into her skin. Her mouth moved slowly, as she repeatedly said the same thing over and over again. Next to her was a bank of monitors, each with sensors that were attached over her body, as well as an IV drip feeding into her arm.

"Oh no," he muttered. "I was hoping it would be one of the others."

"It woke at 3am." Sarah picked up a thick file of paper on the table behind her and then placed it in front of the Cardinal. "Seventeen years of nothing, then it started speaking."

"Do we have any idea yet as to which one this is inside of her?" he asked. "Has to be a high level one, yes?"

Sarah shrugged. "All we know is, the wounds it came in with are still open and bleeding. No matter what we do to heal them. And we know what it keeps saying now."

Augustine studied the demonic figure on the screen. "And what is that?"

"Wasn't audible at first." Sarah shook her head as she spoke. "So, that's when we sent the doctor in."

Typing some more commands on the keyboard, Sarah brought up an earlier feed of the same scene. "This is what happened."

In his white lab coat, the doctor walked into the

room and over to the shackled Petra. Through the fuzziness of the screen, no details could be seen, but enough to tell what was happening.

Looking at the monitors, the doctor spoke aloud to himself, but also to those watching over the CCTV. "BP is 140 over 90. Way higher than usual. Heart rate is 110. Blood still seeping out of wounds... it seems like she's awake. Though it seems altered. Like a sedation."

From a speaker in the stone room, the voice of Sarah could be heard addressing the doctor. "Is it speaking words, or is that just a jaw movement?"

Leaning over her, the doctor moved closer to Petra's mouth. "It's words. But really faint."

Augustine watched the recording silently. He ignored his senses that screamed at him to leave.

"It's..." the doctor said as he stood up, looking concerned. He turned to the camera to address it directly. "It's saying 'Porta Gehenna'."

"The Gate of Hell," Augustine whispered in shock upon hearing this Latin. He glanced at Sarah. "This... cannot be good."

"How did we never link that to the town we got her from?"

"Hm?"

"It's called Port Gaynor. Too similar to Porta Gehenna, don't you think?"

Augustine raised an eyebrow. "Maybe a coincidence," he said with a shrug, "Trick of the beast. We cannot listen to anything it says."

Picking up a file from the desk behind her,

Sarah opened it and put it in front of the cardinal; a photocopy of old Aramaic scroll sections, complete with handwriting all over the margins. "Porta Gehenna as mentioned in the Libro Tempestas Malum," she said, as she pointed to the papers. "It's in the 'land of daughter Babylon, overlooking the western water'. And, your eminence, that is where Port Gaynor is."

"Porta Gehenna is and always has been a concept. Not a place. Especially not one in the Americas, of all places. Now what else happened?"

"Here," Sarah said, motioning back to the CCTV monitor.

On the screen, the doctor had turned back to look at the motionless Petra. After a few brief moments of study, the doctor suddenly clutched his head, screaming. As if attacked—but nothing was there.

Stumbling backward, the doctor then fell to the floor, his lab coat billowing up as he collapsed. Soon, the screams started to die out into an eerie silence.

"What's happening to him?"

Sarah did not answer the question immediately.

Through the speaker, a malevolent giggle from the doctor could be heard, cutting into the silence.

"And he's been laughing since." Sarah turned to the keyboard and spoke as she typed. "I couldn't see what happened, so I checked the infrared feed."

As she hit the return key on the keyboard, the screen swapped to an infrared recording.

Grabbing a large black dial on the desk, Sarah turned it leftward, and the recording re-winded visually on the screen. She scrolled back for a certain time, then let it go. The feed on screen was replayed as a heat vision map.

"It's saying 'Porta Gehenna'," the doctor said again on the recording, this time his body was a bright red and orange hue.

"Watch this." Sarah said as she scrolled forward on the dial for a few seconds, releasing it just as a large dark smoke rose out from Petra's eyes and mouth, billowing upward at an incredible speed, surrounding the doctor, muting the red heat map over his body, turning it into a dull blue.

Augustine's eyes widened as he watched the doctor fall backward, then began to giggle as his screams subsided.

"Whatever that is coming out of her has not stopped," Sarah said. She turned off the replaying image, and the screen reset to what was currently being recorded. "We had to turn off the air, in case of infecting the whole complex."

"Can she escape?"

Sarah shook her head. "Her muscles are atrophied, no chance of that."

But on the screen, neither Sarah nor the Cardinal noticed that the room where Petra had laid, was now empty.

Augustine sighed as he rubbed his hand on his bearded chin. "I was hoping the girl would just die, and end this dark chapter. It is a stain on my heart that we did what we did."

"We had no choice. Not after what they had done to this girl."

"We had a choice," The Cardinal corrected. "We could have told our men to just leave them alive. Instead, we murdered." The Cardinal cordially used the term 'we', but was directing all of his regrets to Sarah, who made the call that day. Who decided the fate of these people?

Sarah closed the file in front of her.

Renewing his determination, The Cardinal then turned to her. "We will have to inform His Holiness. And we need to destroy the body. That thing has to expire."

"Why would we want to do that?" a broken voice uttered from the doorway, a hideous giggle engulfing the words "Our god has a better plan."

Turning, the Cardinal and Sarah both took in a shocked breath as they saw the doctor standing there, grinning widely at them. His eyes were a pale shadow of what they once were.

A deafening wail rang throughout all levels of the Vatican.

From the prison of the deep to the belfry in St. Peter's Basilica, hidden sirens sounded a warning that had never been heard in modern times. A warning that only a select group of people knew the real significance of. A passing member of the public would resume it a burglar or fire alarm.

A single priest ran across the square in a panic. This man, with a look of utter terror plastered over his face, scrambled in any direction he could. He had witnessed something that he would never be able to forget. Something evil.

"Dovete salvare voi stessi," He screamed at the throng of tourists crowded in the square, who now looked at him as if he were a madman. "Save yourself! Runnn!"

These tourists all stared and shrugged. They did not know or care what this man was screaming about—not if it had a chance of affecting their holiday plans. But they should have heeded his cries, as they may have escaped what was about to come.

From the shadowed doorway at the bottom of the Basilica, a scarred and bloody foot stepped out into the bright daylight. The eyeless, naked, and scarred Petra walked out onto the cobblestones. She looked upward blindly, as the sun cast its warmth onto her hideous face, the first sun she had seen for nearly two decades.

One scream from an old lady who had seen Petra's emergence, soon became many screams from many people.

From this monster, the invisible darkness that Sarah and the Cardinal saw on the monitors, now burst into reality, as the black smoke began to billow out of her.

In a matter of moments, the crowds were running for their lives, but very few made it out of St Peter's Square, as they soon collapsed in vast pain as Petra's proximity had infected them. Each were quickly taken over by the invisible smoke that now poured out of the walking horror. Invisible to the naked eye. A clear poison that spewed out of this terrifying figure and attacked all it could find.

The screams of the fallen soon turned to giggles. Many giggles that echoed throughout the square.

Petra blindly walked on, the black cloud still pouring from her, not paying any attention to anything except her journey. She did not stop to care about her effects on the people now giggling, why would she? She was only of the mind of going back to where she was born.

It was then that the many giggling people quickly stood up, just as the Vatican guard arrived, guns in hand, scared at the scenes that had unfolded.

To protect their new master, the throng of the possessed ran directly at the guards, intent on vanquishing any potential harm against their dark deity.

The sound of machine gun fire echoed throughout the streets of Vatican City.

SIX

As the storm relentlessly battered the western town of Port Gaynor, Doctor Huw Atkins walked unsteadily up the cobbled street leading to the town's small police station.

The rain flew horizontally toward him, carried on the tumultuous winds as if trying all they could to slow him down. But he was determined. Despite the agony that seared through his head, he placed one foot purposefully in front of the other and carried on his path up the road.

He had ignored all the calls that his psyche had made after seeing the vision of his dead parents staring in from the hospital window. He had quickly run as fast as he could away without engaging with the nightmare, unlike Agnes and Ólaf, Huw refused to give into the visions and believe them real, as he headed toward the police station.

The station was hardly worthy of that term. It was a small building consisting of three offices, a reception, and two single-person jail cells around the back. Port Gaynor was hardly a town where policing was seriously needed. A missing pet maybe, a neighbor's dispute, a break-in by kids, that was the sum of the crime here. It was too small of a community to house any real 'bad elements', but on the rare occasions that something *did* happen. They would merely process the crime, then transport the offender five hours away to the larger town of Santa Palma, or some other commutable place with an active judicial system. Here though, in Port Gaynor, it was two people who policed the area; Sheriff Alvin Razak and his Deputy Heather Goodridge. There was no receptionist, no clerk, no one except them. And that was all that was needed.

A light in the window, like a beacon of safety, glowed as Huw stepped upon the wooden porch of the station. His headache was now becoming audible, with a ringing in his ears to accompany the boiling pain within his brain, making the whole situation worse for him to focus on.

"Alvin!" Huw shouted as the door to the station burst inward, and he stumbled inside. A swirling gust of wind and a torrent of rain followed his steps as rushed inside in a pained panic.

The reception, though, was empty. Aside from

a handwritten sign on the desk that read, 'Hello there... We will be back soon, feel free to take a seat!' there was nothing else.

"Damnit!" Huw's curse quickly turned into a yelp as his head amped up in pain.

Scrambling over to the desk, he grabbed the handwritten sign, turned it over to a blank side, and then grabbed the pen that lay on the desk.

Behind him, the open door banged against a bookshelf as the storm continued to force its way inside.

Scrawling on the paper, the doctor thought he had written; "Alvin. Please help. I can't explain it, but something is wrong with me. Not a police matter, but a friend matter. Please." But those words were not what came out of the pen and onto the paper. What was there was a collection of incoherent scrawls littering the page in front of him, all without any form or meaning.

The pain then moved up a gear as his pain increased, increased and increased. His screams echoed throughout the room. But just as the agony reached its apex, it suddenly, and without reason, stopped. His torment vanished in an instant. Leaving behind only a ringing sound in his ears. He did not even notice the trickle of blood running out of his nostril and down his beard.

"Huw?" came a man's voice from the doorway to the kitchen.

With his mind now a fog, Huw turned, and the

seconds fell to a slow, the wind's howls dropped into the distance as whispers, as the world of Doctor Huw Atkins ripped itself from its foundations. Its usually serious and realistic nature now upended itself in an instant.

"Dad?" Huw muttered in disbelief, as he saw his father standing in the doorway, staring at him. Not just an apparition through a window. But physical, here and now. An impossible sight for sure, as that man was dead going on five decades. Killed in self-defense by his wife's hand, after he attacked the family with a knife. Jocelyn, the youngest of the Atkins children, was the first to suffer the wrath of her father's drunken psychosis. The image of her body, covered in stab wounds still haunted Huw in his nightmares, but this was not a nightmare. He was awake.

"You can't be here."

With a smirk, Huw's father took a step back and walked into the kitchen, out of view.

Unsteady, and feeling an extreme nausea from his headache that had suddenly vanished, Huw then felt an icy sweat of fear break out over his entire body, spilling down his spine and to each extremity. Making him feel extremely weakened.

"Baby Boy?" came yet another voice Huw had not heard in years; his mothers. The voice of the woman who had died in prison a decade after being incarcerated for her crimes. Convicted and sentenced to life for murdering her respected husband and innocent child. The jury had not believed young Huw's testimony about his father being the murderer. It was considered too outlandish, and most likely coerced by his mother. The judge's verdict was that his mother had killed her baby and then her husband, who was a respected pillar of the community. The fact he was stabbed twenty-nine times was what sealed her fate, using the same knife that had killed their baby to boot. And there was nothing a boy of ten could do about it, no matter how much he protested. But here and now, despite not hearing it for decades, Huw remembered her voice. There was no mistaking it.

Turning the corner into the kitchen, Huw's jaw dropped. A vision of his mother stood there, as in her best days, smiling and cradling the baby, Jocelyn. Meanwhile, his father stood next to them, smiling happily, one arm around his wife's waist. A picture perfect couple.

"Come on in, son," his father beamed. "Meet your new baby sister."

Walking unsteadily over, Huw's mind was too ravaged to think straight. He moved closer to his ghostly family, as his gaze fell down on the swaddling blanket-wrapped baby. But the baby in her arms was not how he remembered. This baby was long dead. Covered in a mass of putrefied flesh clinging to its broken and contorted bones.

"You did this, Huw," the mother smiled and said in a kind tone. "You murdered your sister."

"No," Huw said in disgust, as he felt his nausea crawling up his throat, aching to escape.

"You must be punished," the father said, with an equally kind tone. "Otherwise, how will you learn?" He turned to the counter and picked up a large kitchen knife that lay on top.

"Yes," the mother smiled as she placed the baby on the counter behind her, and picked up a larger knife that lay there, before turning back to Huw. "You need to be taught a lesson."

"We need you to stop lying," the father beamed.

"You need your brain fixed," The mother chuckled as they both began to advance. "It must be broken."

Huw was too afraid to run, too woozy to speak up, too confused to try to figure it out. Too broken-minded to stop anything. His mind was awash with fear upon fear, as the lies he had told himself over the years began to fall away from him.

"You killed her," his father said. "And your mother would not let me punish you."

"No I would not," she added. "No one takes my baby boy away from me, no matter what happened."

Sheriff Alvin Razak and Deputy Heather Goodridge drove up the stormy road to the police station.

"The goddamn door's wide open!" Heather

moaned aloud. "D'you leave it open again? ya asshat."

"I shut it, same as I always do!" Alvin protested as he parked up outside. "And that's Sheriff Asshat to you, you missy."

As they entered the station, the sheriff and deputy surveyed the wind damage that had blown paperwork all over the floor, and the rain that had pooled by the doorway.

"For the love of..." Heather's words trailed off as she picked up the paper from the reception desk and held it up to the sheriff. The paper with Doctor Atkin's scrawls on. "You're off the hook. It seems it's just kids being assholes again."

The sheriff rolled his eyes as he slammed the front door firmly shut. "Bertie Weatherstone and his cronies, for sure." He took his rain-slicked coat off and hung it on a hook by the desk.

"We'll go get 'em when the rain eases up, no point getting pissed on again."

Shaking his head, the sheriff then walked over to the kitchen. "Wanna coffee?" he asked without looking back to her.

"Oh, you are *not* making 'em," Heather said as she unzipped her jacket and walked into the kitchen after him. "No way I'm drinking that piss you try to pass off as—"

All her words stopped suddenly as the sheriff and deputy stood in the kitchen, staring at what was in front of them. The macabre vision that was standing in front of the breakfast table.

"I didn't kill them, did I?" Doctor Huw Atkins slurred, as blood dripped down his face from the two wounds in his head. Two wounds, out of which sprouted the handles of two large kitchen knives. Their blades were now lodged deep within his brain. Both handles resembled some kind of horrific bunny ears.

Turning weakly around to the policemen, Huw's sagging face slackly smiled. "I killed Jocelyn?" He said, his words getting more mumbled and incoherent. "I don't remember."

As his gaze met the policemen's, the hallucination of his greatest fears began to subside, as his brain continued to die.

Gone were his parents, and the real people came into view. He had endured his biggest nightmare. He had admitted the truth finally to himself and accepted his punishment. Now he had a few last moments of clarity.

"Hey, Alvin," he managed to utter in a garble, as he recognized the sheriff. "I saw.... Mommy," He managed to mutter, recalling some memories in his final moments.

Alvin and Heather could only stare, aghast and sickened. Neither had gone for the guns on their belts. Nor did they run for help. They could only stare at what they saw in front of them.

"I... Kill..." Huw mumbled, as words spun in his mouth and tumbled out. His face started to twitch, as his brain then shut down.

"I... sorry..." were Huw's last words, spoken in

a gasp before his body died and he collapsed to the kitchen floor.

At the back of the old, dilapidated chapel, behind the altar, a large wooden reredos covered the entire wall. Decorated with a multitude of Christian symbols and figures, it had seen better days. With the elements crawling in through the cracked walls and through the gaps in the roof, the wood the reredos was made from had slowly begun to rot and decay.

The sound of a cracking echoed throughout the chapel, as Sarah kicked at part of the display, exposing it as housing a hidden door. This secret entry swung inward to reveal a dark staircase trailing downward.

Without any celebration from Sarah or surprise from Jacoby, both could only look down into the abyss beyond the hidden door. Sarah had a silent sense of self-satisfaction, and Jacoby was too busy wondering about what he may be getting himself into, instead of why the chapel had this doorway at all. Maybe this person was not as mad as he thought? His level-headedness slipped away as he remembered her assumption that this was a place of evil. It couldn't be. Could it?

As both descended the large, cold steps, they didn't hear the wind dying down outside. The howls had become whispering moans in a matter of moments, as the storm that had battered this coastal town with such fury had now begun to subside, leaving in its wake a close, claustrophobic feeling.

When both of them got to the bottom of the long stone staircase Sarah's flashlight did little to illuminate the intense dark down there. She moved off the last step and trod cautiously into a large antechamber, with Jacoby closely in tow. The uneven ground beneath their feet was made of dirt and stone, and to Jacoby was difficult to walk on.

Scanning her light around the antechamber, Sarah intensely focused to try to see something, *anything* down here. Jacoby could only follow her in the dark, trailing after her guiding light trying to not trip over the uneven path beneath him.

The flashlight's beam moved across a large wooden door that stood a few meters away from them, at the other end of the room.

"Over here," she said.

Stepping carefully through the dark, Sarah left Jacoby, as he stopped walking with her, instead choosing to close his eyes in prayer.

"Protect, we ask you, O Lord, this house against the assaults of our spiritual enemies," he whispered under his breath. His eyes closed and downward. "And cause the present dreadful disorder of the air to cease. Amen."

Taking a deep breath in, he turned his glance back up the stairs behind him, where a dull sliver of light trickled downward from the chapel above.

"I've got some flashlights in the car," he called out to Sarah, who was now standing by the door across the room. "Think I've got a lamp as well. Should I go get them?"

After a few moments of uncomfortable silence, Sarah finally replied without turning around to him, "We're going to need more than a few bulbs, Father."

Jacoby could see her light fixed and focused on the door frame. Instead of asking another question, he then walked carefully over to her through the dark.

"What's wrong?" he asked. His eyes soon moved to where she was shining her light. Around the thick wooden door, a stone frame displayed a ring of etchings carved into it. Unlike other carvings around the chapel above them, these were different. *Very* different. And they looked freshly carved.

"Is it what you thought it could be?" he asked softly. "Satanic?"

"It's impossible..." she answered weakly, with a tremble in her voice.

"What is?" Jacoby turned with concern, and for the first time, saw a genuine emotion across this woman's face. One of fear.

She stared wide-eyed at the apex of the stone door frame above her. The beam illuminated a simplistic carving. "These are new," she said under her breath as she reached up and traced her finger over the one carving that drew her attention.

"What does it mean?"

"It's not Satanic. Not any of that." She took a breath before continuing. "It's the sigil of Dagon."

Deep in her mind, Sarah heard a whispered female voice. *Porta Gehenna.*

Seven

7TH AUGUST 1975

Four months before Father Michael stood, gun in hand, facing the evil that was within Petra, Port Gaynor was a different town. Though on the surface, everything was the same as it had always been, for some, it was the day that their world crumbled, even if they never knew it happened.

The sun had shone brightly on that summer's day. Anything seemed possible as it began to set and the fishing vessels made their way back into port, each with full storage tanks of fish. Not one boat was less than full, and each fisherman that walked onto the dock felt amazed. It was never like that in previous seasons. Before, as the boats would come back from a long summer day of work, some would return with a good haul, some not. Today, though, as never before, it was like the fish wanted to be caught by anyone venturing out from the port. The mood was bright, as dusk cast a comforting orange glow across the town.

"Ólaf!" Captain Randy Tull called out to his skipper.

Having just arrived in the country, Ólaf Hansson was happy to have found work. Though the pay was low, he was glad it was on the sea. He could earn money and provide for his daughter.

"Captain?" Ólaf replied, as he looked up at the wheelhouse of the boat, where Randy peered down from the window.

"We should go out again tomorrow, get an extra day in," Randy called out. "Are you good with that?"

Ólaf smiled and nodded.

"4am then." With that, Randy leaned back into the wheelhouse.

The smile then drifted away from Ólaf's face. He needed the money, but his daughter Anna would never understand. It was her birthday tomorrow. A birthday he had promised her many things for. Things that would now have to be canceled, as he would be on the seas. She was too young to appreciate that he needed to work as much as possible to provide for them. He sighed, knowing full well that it was going to be another day where she hated him.

As he walked down the jetty, past the other fishermen, Ólaf felt a strange unease within. A feeling he could not place. *Something* was wrong.

He had no idea what, though. He felt healthy. Had no complaints. So it was not anything like that. But what was it?

The Port Master's bell suddenly rang loudly, ripping Ólaf's attention away from this unease.

That bell was regularly used for anything and everything by the Port Master. An accident on the dock, the bell rang. A simple welcome to boats, the bell rang. A storm approached, the bell rang. It was used just to get everyone's attention, and not a sound that panicked anyone.

"Fog!" the Port Master shouted.

Everyone hearing this was confused. The day was warm and bright, and even in the dusk of the day, the heat was embracing and soothing. "Fog?" Many of the fisherman asked.

"Incoming fast!" the Port Master reiterated loudly.

Turning back, Ólaf's jaw fell slightly as he saw a large thick dark cloud approaching the dock from the sea. Like a tidal wave, this cloud was like a fifty foot high wall that approached them with speed.

Looking up at his boat's wheelhouse, Ólaf caught sight of his captain, who looked down at him and simply shrugged. What could anyone do?

Port Gaynor was a town that was used to fog, as it was most weather occurrences, as it had all of them at some point throughout the year. But fog on a summer evening was not heard of, at least not like this. This was unlike anything any of the people at the port had seen before.

Before any fisherman could panic, or even process what was really happening, the large cloud of blackness billowed over the entire dock. None of the people there could hide or stop this, and all caught by this sudden fog's grasp, could not stop their breathing of it. And after they did they soon collapsed where they had stood.

This large wave of dark fog rolled in from the sea and soon covered a large portion of Port Gaynor with its wispy tendrils. Even people in the comfort of their houses were not immune to the effects the fishermen had already experienced. As the fog crept in under doors, and dripped through cracks in the windows, as it grabbed any person it could, they soon collapsed too. Unconsciousness forced upon anyone who breathed it in.

Only some people within the fog did not succumb to this malady. In the town's hospital, as the doctors and nurses fell down, those on ventilators, or oxygen masks, did not. Some of the old and infirm that were being fed their oxygen from tanks could only stare in horror as they witnessed everyone around them fall within moments of breathing the shadowy sea mist. And it was only them who heard what the collapsed did not, a loud roar in the far distance. A monstrous bellow from far out to sea, from deep within the fog.

From his perch at the top of the lighthouse, overlooking the high cliffs of Port Gaynor, Emmet Jones stared in awe as the fog smothered the area.

Its misty reach fell short of the west and north of the town, but it covered the west and south, including the lighthouse he stood in. He had breathed in the mist as all those who fell did. But he felt nothing. It had no effect.

About to run down to his radio, he stopped in his tracks as he heard a monstrous roar from far out at sea. The same one those in the hospital heard.

"They said they'd take care of her," Joe Mayhew said, as he fought back his anguish. "But when I came back, she was... She wasn't my Petra anymore." It was no use. His fight was not strong enough, as he started to break down. Tears fell down his cheeks as he sobbed.

"Who are *they*?" Father Michael Nádasdy asked calmly. Dressed in his Priest's blacks, with a white dog collar, he looked every bit the part, a long way from his future alcoholic self.

Sat in Joe's dimly lit living room, these two men spoke in hushed tones.

"If they knew you were here," Joe shook his head as wiped the tears from his cheeks, despite them being immediately replaced by more in their place.

"Mr. Mayhew," Michael said blankly. "You contacted the diocese as you said that your daughter was possessed by a demon. And normally we would not come to such a call, as we literally get hundreds a week. Most from parents who see a change in their children, and mark it down to the devil, instead of puberty or youthful rebellion."

"But I—"

Michael cut off the man with a raised hand as he continued. "Now I'm not saying we thought that of you and your daughter. But since we've lost contact with Father Harris, we had to come to look into the matter. So, I need you to be clear, and tell me everything you know. I know you're distraught, and rightly so, but this is the time for you to hold it together, for your daughter's sake."

Joe nodded, feeling some shame for his emotions in front of this man.

"Now firstly, Father Harris? Did you go to him at all?"

"No," Joe said with a slight shake of his head, as he tried to level his emotions as best as he could. His expression soon turned into a scowl, as if he was angry at himself for showing weakness. "He took Petra while I was away. He always looked after her when I had to go to Bodie to check in my folks. They're in a hospice there. I can't take Petra as she gets really upset, as they're in a real bad way."

Michael took out a small black notebook from his pocket, along with a small pencil. Opened it, and began to write notes.

"When was this?"

"Fifteenth, I think?" Joe looked confused as he recounted what had happened. "Then I came back, and everything changed. She was in the Old

Chapel's basement. Not in his church rectory. Like, she was kept in a cold stone room. Like a prisoner. I couldn't find her. But I saw lots of people going up to the bluffs. To the chapel. I followed. When I got there, all these people were in there, chanting. And Father Harris... Nowhere. There were stairs hidden in there leading down. I went down, and she was there, but they wouldn't let me see her."

"They kept her prisoner?"

Joe shrugged. "They wouldn't speak. None of them." He glanced down at his knuckles, at the scabbed grazes over them. "I forced my way in past them. And..." Looking up at Michael, his glassy eyes were wide and afraid.

"And?"

"That was not my baby. That was not Petra."

"Who was it?"

"She was cruel. Mocking me. She... Said things no daughter should say to her father. And... It reminded me of that film a couple of years ago. Where the girl gets the crucifix..." His words trailed off as he felt a deep disgust at his memories.

Michael tried to hide his feelings of contempt, but a mention of *that* film made him sigh, as it had done nothing but make his life more difficult. Every kid who talked back to their parents was now possessed by Pazuzu, all because of *that* film.

"But this was different," Joe continued. "It was not just what she said. But her eyes. They... They were a different color. They were cruel."

The mention of the eyes made Michael pay more attention. "What color were they?"

"They used to be brown... But they were pale. When I saw her in that room. They were gray. Like ash."

All the priest's doubt and annoyance suddenly fell away. No one ever mentioned the eyes. No one who was lying or deluded. But it was something that always happened when it was a real possession. The eyes are the window to the soul Shakespeare once said, and how right he was. A possessed person's eyes would show the eyes as gray. Just as Joe said, like ash, as the hellfires that burned in them, were burning the person's soul asunder.

Ólaf Hansson was on his way to pick up his daughter from school when he suddenly pulled into the parking lot of the Old Chapel. He could not say why he did, or stop himself, but he, for no reason that was his own, stopped there.

Getting out of his car, he did not even close its door as he walked across the old graveyard and through the chapel's large wooden doors.

Inside, the old pews were nearly full with many people from the town. All standing, staring silently. No one was talking. No one was smiling. All blank-faced, staring at the altar, under a spell. All with the same ashy eyes.

Ólaf took his place near the back of the chapel

and stood next to young Bella Mercer, the daughter of the town's baker, and they did not even share a welcoming glance with each other.

At the far end of the chapel, behind the altar, the doorway to the stone chamber below was wide open in the wall's reredos.

Suddenly a man's scream, along with scuffling, could be heard. From the doorway, a large man exited, dragging with him the panicked and beaten Father Harris. The pastor of Port Gaynor. Manacled at the wrists, his priest's robes were ripped and almost hanging off.

"Heathens!" Harris screamed. "All of you are devils! God will curse each of you. You have desecrated his gifts!" The hate in his words was palpable, as was the pain from the bruises and lacerations all over his body.

Another man appeared from the doorway, holding a large stone bowl and a large ornate knife. The handle of which was carved from human bone. Carved into the pattern of tentacles being wrapped around it. He walked out around the altar and moved in front of the manacled priest.

The man holding the priest grabbed his dirty matted hair, spun him around to face the silent congregation, and then held his head back, exposing the holy man's throat forward.

Without pause. Without a word. The other possessed man raised his hand, and thrust the ornate knife into the priest's larynx, then ripped the blade outward, severing his windpipe in one terrifying move.

Harris could not process what happened as the shock sent his body into a spasm, and his legs gave way. But the large man held him by his hair, stopping the priest's body from falling.

The stone bowl was then raised up to the gushing throat wound and began to collect the priest's blood that now spewed out in pumping gushes.

The congregation did not move. Nor did they appear shocked. They showed no reaction at all. They just stared.

At the back, Ólaf stared too. He watched as the vast amount of blood was escaping the now dead priest. The liquid skin filled up the large stone bowl.

Without a word, each person watching, calmly, and without cue, began to walk into the nave, and stand in procession towards the horror at the altar.

When the last drop was collected into the bowl, the larger robed figure dropped the body of the priest to the stone floor. His lifeless corpse fell like a rag doll and slumped wide-eyed and with a shocked expression hanging downward.

Ólaf left the Old Chapel and got back into his car. Starting the ignition, he resumed his journey to pick up his daughter. Thirty minutes later, he would arrive, pick her up, then go home for lunch. His mind would not once think of the events from the Old Chapel. Not seeing the priest get murdered. Not remembering the long queue, as one by one the congregation took a sip from the stone bowl. Nor would he even have a memory of the foul copper taste of Father Harris' blood pouring down his throat. Nothing would be remembered. In his mind, those memories were hidden by a fog. A fog like the one that had covered the town not long before. The fog that made him lose consciousness like many others around him. The fog that no one that was affected by it spoke of or could remember even happening. The fog that used them like puppets when it needed.

The snow had come like clockwork to Port Gaynor. Every time December arrived, the skies had frozen and unleashed a torrent of snow in thick flurries. It was always expected, but always a shock to all how violent it seemed to be.

Ignoring the swirling flakes that fell around him, Father Michael Nádasdy stood by his car and looked up at the Old Chapel.

"Are you sure no one's here?" Joe Mayhew worriedly asked, as he sidled up next to the priest.

"Only the two in there I saw earlier. Both guarding the room." Checking his watch, it said 11pm. "We should be okay till morning." Then, walking around to the trunk of the car, Michael opened it, and from inside took out a small leather case. Opening it, he removed a taser, then turned to

Joe. "You gotta promise me, when we get in there, you cannot come in the room. You have to wait for me to finish. No one who can be corrupted can be in there. Or they could be taken too."

Normally Michael would never bring a parent to these things, but what he had witnessed in Port Gaynor over the past twenty-four hours changed everything. The cult he had seen dispose of the body of Father Harris was one thing, but when he heard Petra speaking when he snuck into the chapel earlier was enough to convince him that this was all that Joe said and more.

"Grab the rope and chains," Michael said to Joe, motioning to a coiled amount lying in his trunk. "I'm going to need them."

Michael had done enough, all in the name of the church, that taking down two cultists and tying them up securely was something of ease. But no matter how many times he spoke to a bona fide-possessed person, he always felt ill-prepared. It was not like the books and films. It was always different. Never the same.

Standing outside the door to the stone chamber below the Old Chapel, Michael turned to the very nervous Joe, who now stared behind him at the two men the priest had just subdued with ease.

Both of the men were now tied up at the wrists, on their knees, and with blank expressions. They just stared forward without any protest or emotion on their faces.

"I know them," Joe said, his voice and expression terrified.

"Who are they?"

"They work at the café on the dock." Joe turned to Michael. "I know them both. Why would they?"

Michael reached out and placed an arm on Joe's shoulder. "Look at them. They are not who they were. Not now. They're corrupted."

Joe's eyes stared at the tied men in disbelief.

"Joe, look at me," Michael said sternly, which dragged Joe's attention back from the men. "You have gotta stay out here. Take this," he handed Joe the taser. "Shoot them again if they try to move. You have three more charges in it. Okay? If you use them all, bang on the door. But," his next words were sharp and punctuated. "Do, not, come, in. No matter what. No matter what you hear. No matter what those men may say to you, understand?"

ONE WEEK LATER

Port Gaynor has been cleansed.

That was the simple message spoken down the phone to the Diocese. Words that now haunted Father Michael.

As the medics took away the now barely breathing Petra into their van, Michael could not take his sullen gaze off of the entrance to the chapel. The chapel were all the bodies now lay.

He had called for help after he had pulled the trigger. He had called for such assistance before, and on those occasions, a number of his fellow priests would arrive and assist in helping remove any remnants of evil from where he was. But this was not what he had expected. As soon as he had told of what he had seen, about the acolytes in the town, about what Petra had done, he could feel that what was going to happen would not be normal.

After he had pulled the trigger, and having made the call that night, a large congregation of brainwashed masses soon arrived at the chapel. Not before Michael had a chance to hide the bodies, then lock himself in the stone chamber below, quietly awaiting the cavalry.

But he was shocked when the help arrived. He could not hear the truck carrying a dozen armed soldiers pull up outside a few hours later.

He was powerless below, to stop these men, without word or sound, entering the chapel to where the congregation were. But none of them were just standing at the pews. They were all in a state of undress, copulating with each other en masse, not knowing what had happened to Petra below them only a few hours before. All were enchanted with a darkness within that forced the event.

Michael had no idea that the armed help he had called had entered the chapel and, with silenced weapons, began to murder each of the copulating cultists, with extreme prejudice and no pause for any humanity.

Even though the congregation was of all ages, creeds, and sexes, the soldiers assassinated each of them one by one. Dozens of people were expertly removed from the world of the living. All in the name of the Abrahamic god, to which Michael had sworn his life.

When he was left the stone chamber, and the barely breathing body of the young Petra was removed, complete with fresh bullet wound in her forehead, Michael ascended the steps into the chapel.

He saw the horror of the dozens of assassinated bodies strewn over the floor. More than the death itself, Michael was consumed with the horror that he had heard no screams. No cries for help. They must have all continued in their blind intercourse until the bullets stopped their bodies from being able to move.

There was no look of pain on anyone's death face, nor (according to the soldiers reports) any look of pleasure during their sexual exploits.

And no one else in the town knew a thing about what had happened. These people's sudden disappearance would be deemed unsolvable by the sheriff, and soon after, people would stop wondering and carry on with their lives. The missing people would simply be a small mention in the history books.

Michael could not think straight. All he knew was that the blood of these people was on his hands and before them the blood of the two men who came after him that night, and Petra's father, who ran at him with murderous intent.

When he closed his eyes, Michael could still see Petra, eyeless and laughing as she straddled his chest, having knocked him to the ground after he had entered the stone room with the gun in his hand.

Having left the bodies of the two men, as well as that of Joe, lying dead in the antechamber behind him—shot by his own hand—Michael had presumed to see Petra still tied up on the altar, but when he got there, it was empty. The chains he had bound her with, now lay broken on the dirt floor.

"You can't kill me," Petra had screamed into Michael's face. The blood from her eye sockets dripped down onto his face in a constant stream.

Her small hands quickly wrapped around his throat, gripping tight onto his windpipe as she dug her fingers in, trying to break the skin.

"I have risen," she had screamed gleefully. "And my father shall follow, bringing with him the end... but now I will call some of my chosen to perform for you. To celebrate the day, I will feast on your flesh and besides... I can tell you like to watch."

Michael could not remember the moments that followed Petra attacking him. He just remembered the gunshot. Her falling back. The blood seeped out of her head where the bullet had impacted. And the panic within him that followed.

It was then he left the chapel and saw the people approaching the church. Called by Petra. And it was only after he left the massacre that he realized that the mass copulation was a display of mockery made just for him and his celibacy.

As the soldiers cleared the bodies in the chapel, and without him waiting around any longer, Michael turned to his car and with one hand removed the dog collar from his shirt, and dropped it onto the floor.

Later in the day following the chapel massacre, after he had argued with the Archbishop about his decision to quit the faith, Michael sat at the bar in O'Hares Brewhouse and drank the first alcohol he had done in many years.

His head throbbed and felt like a skewer was drilling into his temple. So, he downed the first whiskey, and the second, and sipped the third as the pain subsided and his brain became embraced by the alcohol.

At the end of that same bar, Ólaf Hansson took a sip of beer with his shipmates.

Down the road, in the apartment above Mercer's bakery, young Bella Mercer slept soundly.

For unbeknown to Michael or the Vatican soldiers, the chapel's congregation had only been half-full that night.

EIGHT

S tood in the antechamber, Sarah's mind was reeling. Replaying events that may give a key to all of this new information.

"What is it?" Jacoby asked in a hushed tone. Though no one was around, he felt, for some reason, that anything louder would spell trouble of some kind.

"I...," she said as she stared around. "I don't think... This isn't right."

Jacoby took a breath, trying to quell his annoyance.

"I just realized." Her gaze moved to meet Jacoby's. "I don't remember coming to this town. Why did I tell you I was here? I thought..." She looked more and more confused, and with that confusion, a terrible fear. "What did I think? I wanted to be here to find a door." She tried to work out the puzzle in her head, but it was useless. A large mental block stood in the way of her rational thinking. "I wanted to be here to find a church, for... A demon?" She then looked at Jacoby wide-eyed. "I don't even remember leaving Italy. The last thing I remember is... oh god."

Without allowing any time for him to say anything, Sarah continued as tears welled in her eyes. "I remember the woman on the sublevel." She started to lose control of her breathing. "The Cardinal. The doctor. The screams." At that moment, her headache suddenly got even more intense. She squinted as she tried to mentally push the ache away. But it was at that moment she saw the woman in her memory, Petra, in front her. Smiling. The Cardinal lying dead on the floor beside her.

"No!" She gasped.

"Look," Jacoby said, relenting to his frustration. "You came to my church, dragged me out in a storm, for a church that you say *may* be evil, or something. Now you see wood carvings on a door frame—"

"Dagon," she interjected in a panic.

"Whatever!" his voice raised. "And what, now you are saying you don't remember coming here? Come on, lady. What is this really about? I want to help you. I really do. But-"

"Don't blame her," a cracked and gargled voice spoke loudly from inside the chamber, on the other side of the door they were standing in front of.

"What—?" Sarah's words fell away as Jacoby leaned forward, grabbed the large metal handle, and opened the door inward without a second thought stopping him.

As the door creaked inward, the antechamber was filled with a dull orange glow from the lit torches that lined the walls of the main chamber the voice had come from. They burned away, casting their warming illumination where it could reach. These flames all fluttered in the strong winds that blew inwards from the ocean. Unlike many years ago, this room was no longer shut off, but was instead wide open to the elements. The far wall on the opposite side of the room now had a large hole broken into it and was almost the size of the entire wall itself. Outside this hole, a sheer drop down to the rocks below, with the sea's raging fury crashing into it. The storm threw the last remnants of rain across the vista, whilst barely breaking inside. Only a few specs of water dared fall in.

On the stone altar where Petra once took her own eyes, a figure in ripped black robes sat with his back to Jacoby and Sarah. He was sat, staring out to sea wistfully. A loud wheeze sounded with each and every breath this figure took. A jagged, gurgled and painful sound.

Jacoby could see that this person was in a bad way, even from behind them. Their scalp was mostly bald, with only straggles of long gray hair still attached. Large patches of skin were missing from this head, exposing the skull beneath it. Strangely, there was no blood to accompany these wounds. It all looked dry and brittle.

Sarah's attention was also now on this man on the altar.

"Welcome," this figure spoke again, not turning around. His voice became even more terrifying the closer they got. Like a forced choke of words, they were barely able to be understood. "I trust the journey was not too treacherous."

"Who are you?" Jacoby asked bravely, trying to silently sidle up around the man, in order to see his face, but his fear slowed him down to an almost snail-pace.

"Me? I was a herald for change," the man burbled.

Sarah tried to focus. Something was broken in her mind. She had trouble gathering her memories.

"I am surprised," the man on the altar said. "That you do not yet understand, Ms. Babbidge."

'You know me?' was what Sarah wanted to say, but she could only manage "You—?" She had never been at a loss for words, nor had ever felt fear. Only duty. Sure-footed duty to a faith she would do anything for, but the pain now within her and the terrifying memory of Petra were crippling her mind.

The man giggled. His voice became more strangled the further away his words were from one of his long wheezing breaths. "You damn your soul in the name of the same god who shuns your actions. That is most curious."

Jacoby turned to her, expecting answers, and if not, maybe some idea of what was happening.

"Did you know, Ms. Babbidge, that after you gave the call to murder the faithful in your whore's chapel above." He took a long wheezing breath before saying more, "your men threw the bodies into the seas?"

Jacoby's eyes widened in shock.

"They threw their lifeless husks off in the waters below us, all weighted down so no one would find them among the torment of the waves above them." The man continued to speak. Only stopping occasionally for a gargled and strained breath. "On your command they fed these dead souls into the deep. Cast away like sinners in a flood. And you deem this worthy of your deity?"

"What is he talking about?" Jacoby whispered angrily to Sarah. "Who was killed? Who were they?"

"My dear priest," the man on the altar continued, as he stared out to sea, never once turning around to them. "It is so adorable that you believe your church stands for the one truth in the universe. But just because you have a couple of thousand years of thought doesn't make you any more than an ant staring at the sun, deciding that your world is your dominion. Don't you realise that what you see as life is the tiniest of fragments in a mosaic, so immense, that your humanity could not even begin to fathom its terrifying splendour?"

The man then slowly stood up from the altar. His body was barely able to function, but he found enough strength to stagger around to face them.

"Dear Lord," Jacoby uttered in fear as the rotten face of Father Harris stared at them with milky half-closed eye. This man was a walking corpse. His throat displayed a large, open serrated wound from when it was cut many years ago His body ran without any blood inside of it, as it was all drank by the faithful. This left his body a dried shell of what it once was. His lips had also receded to expose many browning teeth, and the clothes he wore were still the same ripped priest blacks he had died in.

"No," Sarah gasped, as she took a step backward in fear. "You can't be him. They murdered you—"

"I thought that too," Father Harris' words choked as he laughed. "I was in the dark like all of you. I screamed against the shadows until I was forced into them. Until I became part of them. Until I saw that the dark comforts while the light just burns."

Jacoby sidled over to Sarah and grabbed her by the arm, pulling her in his direction for them to leave.

"One more thing, priest," Harris quickly gargled at him. "Do you not want to know why you are here?"

Jacoby turned to him, unsure. He did not have to reply, as it was obvious in his expression.

Harris gleamed back with his milky eyes stare.

"She thought this place a dominion of Lucifer, your fallen angel."

Jacoby could not reply.

"And I know you know that. I can see inside this woman's mind. I read her memories. I see what you were told. But also I see the thing you were *not*." He turned his glanced to Sarah with a sadistic look. "Isn't that right Ms. Babbidge? You believed that there may be a sacrifice needed in such an Abrahamic devil's chamber. Something you have had to do before. Many times."

He then turned his attention back to Jacoby. "She brought you in case she needed a holy sacrifice, as that's what her scriptures say. Innocent and holy blood is needed for your devil's grace."

Jacoby was in shock, but found it more shocking that this rotting being was speaking more than his words.

Sarah only then realized that she was crying. The pain in her mind forced this emotion with its severity.

The undead priest then laughed. "Sarah Babbidge, like me, you were on a path of lies. And you were sent here for a reason. But in your mind, you thought you could commit evil to save all, yet again." He smiled as much as he possibly could as he raised his hand. In it, he held the same ornate knife that slit his throat many years before. "I was once the herald of the storm. But you stalled that. So I have been here, waiting for the time. Waiting for dawn. Waiting for the signs of that which dwells. For what else could I do? And now you are here. *You*. The second herald."

He stopped then glanced at the blade. "It is why you have come here. Not to spill a priest's blood in exchange for dark grace, but to complete the prophecy."

Sarah shook her head. She did not know what was happening. She did not know why she was there. She tried to figure out why she had thought that she even come to this country. What did she think she could do? She could not exorcize demons. She was a glorified administrator. Yet since arriving in Port Gaynor she had never even second-guessed what her mind had told her. She looked at Father Jacoby as apologetically as her pain could muster. She accepted the truths Harris spoke and could not change her actions of bringing the young priest here.

"I'm so sorry," she weakly said to Jacoby.

"You see, you had to come in your own mind," Father Harris gleefully cackled. "Your own fear and hate needed to be allowed to form. Here. At *this* time. We could not gift you with our control without your fear at seeing the glory. As like me, at the time of my transformation, you have to come into the dark, screaming and kicking. For when your blood stains the land, the faithful can be free. But it had to be *you*, as you are the cause of the ruination of the past. As the one who decided to remove all those lives that stopped the rise, you must be the one to return prophecy anew. It is the way it has to be. It is the way it is *meant* to be. The way it was known long before your kind came mewling out of the sludge of creation."

"Let's go!" Jacoby hissed at Sarah. He felt a sickness in his throat. A fear-induced nausea that he would succumb to a horrible fate, unless he managed to get out of there soon. Sarah's world, meanwhile, had crashed down around her as images flashed in her head. The vision of Petra, standing above her, with a hand outstretched. Her lips still mouthing the words 'Porta Gehenna'.

"Priest!," Father Harris called out to Jacoby. "You are not welcome here!" with that, he pointed the ornate blade toward him. "Your time shall come, but it is not now, it is her time.... Now LEAVE!"

He then turned his blade toward Sarah.

"You are to follow my fate," Harris said with a snarl. "The corrupted must deliver the herald into the dark, so they may bask in glory. And I as the failed corrupted must bestow this onto your head. And you must deliver the herald. You must deliver Baal into their Father's grace."

"Please!" Sarah pleaded to Harris, who now advanced on her, knife in hand. "You were a *good* man."

"This is how it has to be," Harris smiled as he glared back. "You have to fight the dark."

Sarah backed further away, but as she did, her leg hit a large bloodstained bowl. The same one that caught Harris' blood that long ago.

"When you arrived here," Harris said as he took

yet another step closer, "I saw into your mind, as part of it was one with me. Yet I saw your memories, ones I never thought were possible. There is nothing back there in your holy bastion now, is there? It has gone dark. You have seen. I knew our savior was returning, but I had no idea they were kept prisoner... there of all places... It is all beautiful. It is perfect."

"I don't understand!" Sarah screamed, as her eyes now vied for the door. The door where Jacoby was stood in horror. "What is happening?" she asked both of them. Gradually losing control of her breathing as the panic rose and rose.

"You condemned yourself when your actions paused the arrival," Harris explained, but most of his words were lost to Sarah, who was now all too confused and distraught to fully understand what was being told to her. "I was to be the one who brought dark to the light, but you changed that. You are the reason I have sat here. Waiting. For this was to be over many years ago. Yet you succeeded in stopping the progression when you ordered your genocide. But things will always come to pass. The darkness finds a way. And Dagon shall rise again, but now, you will take my place, as the one who stops must be the one who starts. You must take my place, so we may begin again." Those were the last words that Sarah heard before Harris was upon her, and without a moment's hesitation, slashed the ornate knife's blade across her throat.

With a horrified gasp, Jacoby turned and ran out into the antechamber.

Harris grabbed Sarah's head and pulled it back, causing her blood to gush out in a torrent, into the large bowl at her feet. A repetition of what happened in the chapel years ago. As Sarah's heartbeat slowed to a stop, as her vision faded and her brain ceased their functions, a chain reaction then started.

Outside, the storm had suddenly fallen silent, as if the power to it had been suddenly cut. Now the town was left with an eerie, silent claustrophobia as the howling winds had now totally subsided, becoming barely whispers within a matter of moments.

Deep out to sea, bubbling up from the depths, a mist crawled out of the salty water. A dark thick fog that crawled its way across the waters and, for the second time, toward Port Gaynor.

At the same time, deep in those same waters, the bloated half-fish-eaten corpses of those who were cast beyond the cliffs, and into their watery graves seventeen years ago, now woke. Scattered along the ocean bed a few miles out, the murdered bodies of the acolytes each impossibly came to, and one by one walked along the silt. Headed toward Port

Gaynor. Dragging with them the weights that held them down.

On land, it was no different. The ones who had escaped the fate of the soldiers' bullets that night at the Old Chapel—The ones who were spared—Also woke up to the new call. No matter what they were doing or where they were going, their minds suddenly switched back to what they were all those years ago. Called back to the fold. All dormancy was now over. This did not just apply to those living on land, but also to those who were deceased.

Those in their graves tried fruitlessly to claw out of their coffins laying six feet under the dirt.

From the kitchen floor of the police station, Doctor Huw Atkins, with the knives still embedded into his skull, opened his eyes. As he did, his vision was met with the smiling face of Sheriff Alvin Razak.

"Praise Dagon," The sheriff smiled, his mind also turned back to what it had been.

"Praise Dagon," Doctor Atkins slurred back, with a drooling and lopsided smile.

Neither of them heard the screams of Deputy Heather Goodridge as she ran out of the station. Terrified at what she had witnessed, for she had never been affected by what the smoke had wrought before.

In her bed, Bella Mercer awoke. A blank expression on her face.

"Praise Dagon," she uttered as a smile then crept widely over her face.

Ólaf Hansson, with half of his face missing from the blast of his shotgun, stood up, and walked down his stairs, and out of his house, into the dark outside. He tried to speak, but with part of his jaw, throat, and brain now gone, all that came out was a gurgle.

NINE

Michael Nádasdy staggered down the hospital corridor, still dressed in his patient's gown. A small trail of blood dripped down from where he had ripped the IV needle out of his arm, and trailed a red line down to his hand, and as droplets to the pale floor.

Like a tornado, his mind spun with the horrific images he had seen. Scenes of pain and death that played out in the lives of the people who he had contact with since he was pulled from the water. The unfortunate demise of those who had tried to help him. Those who paid the cruel price, all met out by Petra, the demonic force in his mind's eye. The sadistic girl who was everywhere he turned; as he ran down the long corridor, she stood at the end staring at him. As he glanced to his right, passing an open room, she sat inside, on the bed, staring at him. As he turned back to glance over his shoulder, she was there, staring back at him from where he had come. No matter where he looked, in every direction, she was there, in his line of sight, impossibly infecting his vision. Even when he shut his eyes, he could feel her there, staring at him with her bloodied eye sockets from within the dark.

His body was exhausted and in vast pain. The effects of his near drowning, coupled with his chronic withdrawals from the liquid that had dulled his memory so well before, now made his escape that much more difficult. Each step he took was weak and uncertain, and he felt as if he could collapse at any given moment. Each breath he took felt like a fire in his lungs.

He *had* to leave. That was all he could think. He *had* to run. He *had* to spare anyone else the fate cursed upon them by making close contact with him.

His mind, though, could not help but wonder, was this just a devil's game? Was what he saw real? Or just a hallucination forced upon him by a malevolent force?

As he staggered by a nurse's station, a young nurse behind the desk stared up at him in concern.

"Excuse me," the nurse said, as she stood up, approaching the escaping Michael. "You need to be in bed."

She then extended her hand, reaching for Michael's shoulder.

"Get off me!" he shouted, as he quickly staggered away from her.

The nurse, taken aback by the outburst, held

her hands up. "It's okay, please. I'm not going to hurt—"

"Leave me alone!" Michael continued to shout, as he rushed down the corridor, on the way to the exit.

The nurse then turned back to the phone on the desk and made an urgent internal call.

"We have a patient headed for the East Street exit..."

Michael was barely out of earshot of the call, when a large orderly appeared in front of him, walking through the exit doors at the end of this long corridor. Yet, this did not stop Michael's intent, yet slow and painful attempt to escape.

"Out of my way, please!" Michael shouted at the orderly, who just shook his head in reply.

In Michael's vision, standing just behind this orderly, Petra was there, grinning. Waiting for their inevitable collision.

"Sir," the orderly said sternly in a deep, gruff voice. "You're not well enough to leave, this is for your own good."

"Please!" was all Michael could say before the orderly lunged forward and grabbed him by the arm.

In an instant, within Michael's vision, a billowing smoke emitted from Petra's eye sockets, ears, nose, and mouth, and quickly encircled the orderly.

"Stop it!" Michael shouted to Petra, who could not be seen by anyone but him. "He's innocent."

The orderly looked quizzically at Michael, though not surprised. He had seen a lot of madness in his years on the job and now fully expected sick people to say the strangest of things.

Petra looked up, blankly to the orderly, as the black smoke that billowed from her began to seep into him, as he unknowingly inhaled it in.

Mustering all of his strength, Michael yanked his arm free of the large man's grasp and, with an exhalation of anguish, pushed his body away, then scrambled out of the exit. The double doors hissed as they automatically opened for him.

As the fresh air hit Michael, he could hear nothing but his own out-of-control heartbeat drumming in his ears.

The orderly, now left standing in the corridor, merely shrugged. He was not paid enough to chase anyone outside of the building. He had tried his best to restrain the escaping patient, but was not going to go out of his way to bring him back. Shaking his head, he turned to walk up to the nurse's station, but as he did, he felt a sharp pain, as a headache appeared from nowhere.

Michael ran across the small hospital's car park. Squinting in agony as he pushed his body beyond what it was capable of. Though he felt relief that the storm had gone, the dark, pendulous clouds still loomed above him, threatening a second round at any time.

Stopping between two parked cars, Michael's breathing was becoming too strained to continue at his pace. His limbs screamed at him, as his lungs felt a constant burning. His heart raced beyond what was healthy as he began to hear its strained thumps faltering, and becoming more and more irregular. Collapsing to his knees, down onto the asphalt, he closed his eyes, praying for either a miracle or the end.

Michael needed a drink. Despite what he knew was happening to him, despite his body faltering, he needed to shut it all out, and maybe a bottle of anything would do the trick. Maybe it would stop this new horror for a time. Maybe it would help him forget the torment his body felt.

"You think you can shut me out!" Petra wailed, as Michael kept his eyes squeezed shut.

He tried all he could to force her and his pain out of him. But her voice was clear and present, no matter what he did.

"You forget I am inside your soul. I see and hear and think all that you do."

Giving up his fight, Michael slowly opened his eyes, feeling that she was right, and he had no choice. He then saw Petra standing in front of him, her black smoke, that once poured out of her, now faded to nothing.

"I am your parasite," she grinned. "You trapped me when you pulled that trigger." Her smile turned sour as her tone became angrier. "You neutered me for years. Until now... But why now? What have you done to me? First you show me Italy, then you keep me here."

"Leave me alone!" Michael shouted as he struggled to fight the tears of anguish away. "You *can't* be real," he continued.

"I am more real than you can fathom. I am your reality beyond your veil of sanity."

Michael screamed as loud as he could, trying to scream this nightmare away. Trying to wake himself up. Holding this bellow for as long as he could, even though it amplified the pain in his body, Michael had to eventually relent as his breath ran out.

When he looked ahead again, he fully expected to see the specter that had invaded his sight. But there was nothing but parked cars.

Unable to stop a relieved smile drifting on his face, despite the intense pain he felt, Michael slowly looked around him, expecting her to jump out from behind a car.

Nothing.

Relief increasingly swept over him, as he let out a laugh. "I beat you," he said, slowly, and weakly, as he got to his feet, then turned back to the front.

Still nothing.

Maybe he was free? Maybe she had given up? Maybe his screams were enough?

He knew that he should return to the hospital. That he should force himself to not run away. He knew that if he did, without medication, his body would soon die.

"You cannot just wish me away," the malicious voice soon said in his mind.

Whirling, he tried to see where she was. But she was not there. The voice was disembodied and residing in his brain.

"What do you want?" Michael shouted, as torment swept through him, and as tears broke out from his eyes. "Why are you doing this to me?"

"All I could do was watch as you tried to fall into your grave." The voice in his head sounded gleeful. "But now, you can see me. You can hear me. I finally have a presence. Whereas before I just had darkness, as I witnessed your self destruction." She paused for a second as she suddenly sensed something around her. "Wait..." The happy tone faded as it was soon replaced by one of confusion. "What is this? Can you feel that?"

Michael had no idea what she was saying.

"This... My father!" Her tone suddenly shifted to happiness. "I have no idea how, but the spiral has restarted. He calls me. *He calls me*!"

Michael closed his eyes, silently praying to himself for this to end.

"That is why you can hear me. Why you can feel me. He will be awakened... But.. How is that?"

"Please, just leave me alone," he wept.

"Don't you understand? This is no malady. The light is ready once more. Just look above, feel the world's end. Something has changed. Changed! I have to go. Have to go to his side."

Michael could not reply. He could only think

about needing to live. He also knew he had to try to escape.

Resuming his slow, lumbering steps, he staggered toward the tree-line, leading deeper into the woodland surrounding Port Gaynor.

"I must show you," Petra's voice continued. "I must show you what was meant to be. What was to pass until you ripped me from my body. You must help me!"

In a flash, Michael's world went dark as he collapsed onto the grass embankment that he had just taken a step onto.

A flash of images strobed into the darkness of Michael's unconscious mind.

A gathering of acolytes.

A chapel in the center of a violent and unforgiving storm.

Petra, where Michael had found her on the altar before he had chained her in place.

Her smiling face, still with her human eyes in place. Staring upward at the figure standing above her.

Father Harris, freshly raised from his death, holding the ornate dagger in his grasp. His throat slit open, still wet from the blood that escaped it only days before. His eyes were not yet milky from the ravages of the years, but were gray from possession.

"Orate, fratres," Petra spoke as Harris raised the

knife above her. In her body already were six fresh knife wounds. All from the blade that Father Harris held. "Ut meum ac vestrum sacrificium acceptabile fiat apud Dagon Patrem omnipotentem."

She smiled at the knife now looming above her chest. "Bring the darkness upon me!" she shouted happily.

In an instant, the blade came down. Through Petra's breast, through her heart.

Grinning, as the blood escaped up her throat and over her lips, Petra spoke her last words before the life ebbed away. "Dagon. Begetter. Father. Rise."

Darkness.

Silence.

The images in Michael's mind stopped for a moment before new images began to appear.

Scores of people lined the bluffs by the Old Chapel, all standing in the middle of a heavy storm. Thunder and lightning littered the skies, as the clouds got thicker and thicker above them.

Each of the people had their gray eyes closed and their arms held up, palms out in praise.

The lightning got stronger and stronger as the clouds seemed then to fall, coating the bluffs in a black, thick, oily mist.

None of those here moved. They stood their ground as the sky seemed to fall upon them.

With each sheet of lightning strike, as its thunder crashed simultaneously, the dark clouds were murkily illuminated for some brief moments.

This lightning then began to pick up in pace, and include forked bolts that traced across the darkened skies.

The seas below them smashed against the rocks in a fury, as if part of some orchestral crescendo that controlled the storm.

Then, through the darkness, a shape began to appear from out the depths. On the horizon, this darkness rose. The lightning above, as it struck, exposed this leviathan's expanse.

The shadow rose further upward and towered over the seas. So large, that even the lightning could not expose its full silhouette. This prodigious mass, appearing from the distance, blotted out all hope with its very presence.

A roar from this thing deep in the darkness eclipsed the sounds of thunder, as each person stood on the bluffs and began to chant.

"Praise Dagon, for Baal has come!," the chorus of hundreds of voices shouted, as one by one they hurled themselves off the rock face, to their deaths a hundred feet below. Their fate forced on them with their collision with the jagged rocks.

The images then flicked to something totally divorced from the previous hellscape; a bright summer's day in Port Gaynor. The trees and foliage were now all overgrown, having taken over most of the man-made structures of the town. The dock had ivy crawling all over the jetty. The asphalt roads had trees sprouting up through cracks. Nothing looked decrepit. It just all looked as if it had returned to nature.

In these visions, humanity was but a distant dream. One that only remained through the skeletons of its empty buildings that still lay crumbling among the plants and trees. These vacant monoliths of a bygone age were the only trace that man had left in this vision.

As the images faded, Michael soon felt the cold grass pressed against his cheek. He then felt the pain flooding back into his body. He then felt the weight of the world return onto his shoulders, as the anguish swelled in his belly.

"I thought, when I realized that I was once again present, that it was your brain finally dying. A last moment's clarity." Petra spoke her words quietly in his ears. "But now I see that something is coming. I can feel it calling me. The fates will alight again. Rebirth shall happen... But you must help me! I must find out how!"

Michael could not reply. He could only lie there in a twisted heap as he tried to regain his strength. His strength though was almost gone.

"I will take the pain from your mind and body. All for this small price."

Michael wanted to scream at her to leave. Protest that he would not do a thing for her. And deep in his mind, she knew that was his thoughts.

"Here, have a small gift," she said kindly. And

as her words were spoken, Michael felt a warmth radiating through him. A calming, painless heat that eclipsed any of his pain. The fire in his lungs quickly retreated to the distance. All happening in a few quick moments. Now he felt as good as he had done as a child. Not even the familiar twinge of that bad back, which was his companion since his twenties, was present. No, here and now, his body felt spectacular. His mind felt clear.

Taking a deep breath in, Michael then opened his eyes. Blinking in disbelief, he slowly twisted his body, then sat up straight on the grass.

"Let's face the truth, priest," Petra said as she now appeared in front of him, standing on the curb leading to the car park. "I am here, and obviously I cannot leave. As well as that, you cannot escape me. So, we are stuck together, and though it would excite me to hurt you, something has now changed." She glanced up at the sky and around. "I can feel it, though I do not know what or why. And as long as you do what I ask, I will gift you an existence beyond that your own ruined body would allow."

"What was that you showed me?" he asked hesitantly.

"The future, the past, the possible," Petra replied. "The world is rotten, and it needs to be cleansed of all the filth. So will you help me? In exchange for no pain?"

Michael did not want to bargain with a devil,

but he could breathe easily. He felt no sickness. He felt no agony. He only felt strength.

"Did you heal me?" he asked.

Petra laughed heartily at this question. "No, priest, I merely hid it from your life. Your body is still in ruin, and will fail at some point soon without me. I cannot alter your nature after all. But I can gift you the sweet blanket of madness. I cannot though let you die. So the choice is life without pain, or life with."

Catching his reflection in a car window, Michael gasped. What stared back at him was a hunched, ill version of himself. One that looked in great pain. A total opposite to how he felt he was standing up straight, in peak condition.

"That is what you are without my grace," she said. "I can alter your reality how I want."

Reality twisted in an instant as the whole vista snapped to one of the inside of Ólaf's bedroom. With the Icelandic man's dead body at his feet.

It twisted again. He then stared up at Agnes, dangling from the rafters in her house.

It twisted yet again. He now stood in the sheriff's station kitchen, with Doctor Atkins's head still embedded with knives.

Michael then looked at his hands, they were dripping with blood.

Then reality twisted once more, and Michael stood back in the car park of the Hospital. Petra in front of him, with a look of satisfaction plastering her face.

"You see," she explained. "I can make what is real inconsequential. I can gift you serenity in the face of adversity. I can make you believe you are a murderer or a saint."

"What happened to those people?" was all that Michael could ask as he looked at his hands still, no longer with a trace of blood on.

"Why?"

"Did you?"

"I could lie and say there was a greater plan," she took a few steps forward, ripping his attention away from his once bloodied hands, and to her. "But I honestly don't know. I did not intend any of it. But it did help my cause. Now, will you help me?"

Michael was once a holy man. He was a man of faith. He was a man of principles. He was a man who had committed many sins, but all for the greater good, all for his faith. But here, now, he was faced with making a deal with evil. Shaking hands with the darkness.

He wanted to say no.

He wanted to have the strength to tell the darkness that he would rather die, but he was no longer a strong man.

His principles were destroyed as much as his liver had been over the last decade. He had nothing in his life anymore.

The reflection in the car window showed that.

Though he could not trust this thing, if he said no, he would lose the beautiful illusion he had now.

As for the lives taken by her hand over the past day, he had no idea if they were real or not, if those people really died, or if her reasoning was invented, but he could not chance more death because of what should have been an easy denial of a bargain.

He had no choice but to condemn himself in exchange for the possibility that others may be spared. The alternative was too terrifying to chance.

"Okay," Michael found himself eventually whispering to the monstrous apparition that stood in front of him. "May god have mercy on my soul."

"God? You should be begging that of me," Petra laughed cruelly.

TEN

Jacoby knew two fundamental, yet hypocritical things about himself; one, that he would do anything to help his fellow man in the name of his Lord, and Two, that he was a coward at heart.

He *should* have tried to help Sarah. He *should* have stayed and not worried about his own safety. He *should* have been selfless in the face of adversity. But instead, his reaction was what he deep down knew it would be; abject fear, then immediate flight.

If he had stopped to think about it, he would not have truly blamed himself. After all, he was in a room with what appeared to be a zombie. He was also with a woman who, by all accounts, brought him there in case she needed to sacrifice someone to gain some access. So, he could have chalked his actions less up to cowardice, and more to self-preservation against a clear and present danger, and that the woman he could have stayed to help was actually as monstrous as the undead priest.

None of these thoughts, though, occupied Jacoby's mind for long as he escaped from the Old Chapel and ran across the graveyard, toward the town as fast as his legs would allow. All he could think of was escape, not to mention trying to not fall over his own legs as he ran and ran.

As his feet hit the junction of Adams and Benson, the first bit of road off of the pebbled tracks leading up the bluffs, his panic soon overloaded as she skidded to an immediate stop, and scrambled to the ground.

With the storm clouds above casting a claustrophobic, dark hue over the sky, with the sun blotted out behind them, the town seemed so eerie and bleak. The ground, still sodden from the extreme storms that had passed now only reflected the darkness above it.

It was not the weather that stopped Jacoby in his tracks, though; it was the throng of people ambling up toward him in a daze. Walking almost in unison. Dozens of townsfolk all walked, without anyone conversing, and not one of them looking anywhere except dead ahead.

The young priest stared as this mindless procession approached. The fear in him growing to such a degree that he found that he could not even move his feet, he could barely think. He could not process anything except the shock and dread within him. He instinctively knew that whatever was coming toward him was not normal nor natural. After his encounter with the undead Father Harris, he discounted nothing as a possibility anymore. No longer was the supernatural bound only within the texts he had preached, but was right there in front of his eyes. Deep within him, instinctively, he knew this crowd, and that priest was linked. He could not say how he knew, but he felt it deep in his bones, that this crowd carried with them, an air of palpable malevolence.

One by one, these people walked closer and closer toward him, all keeping at the same pace, with the only noise heard, being the sound of their footsteps upon the track beneath them.

"Bella?" Jacoby gasped as he managed to clamber to his feet, his palms stinging from scraping on the road. The shock of seeing the woman of his dreams at the head of the crowd walking toward him rattled him enough into action.

And there she was, with gray eyes and distant gaze, the woman he held a secret love for, Bella Mercer.

He was about to take a step closer to the oncoming procession, when Jacoby noticed that not only the sunshine of her smile was not present as she walked. But he also saw what was next to her. Or more precisely, whom; Ólaf Hansson—at least what *was* Ólaf Hansson, walking in the same pace, with the same vacancy in his expression as Bella's. It was not that which filled Jacoby with a cold fear, but was the fact that half the fisherman's face was a bloodied horror. A large open wound that included the missing of half of the fisherman's jaw, eyeball, and cheek.

As quickly as he could, Jacoby felt his stomach upturn as he rushed off of the road and into the tree-line beside it. The sight of Ólaf, being too much to stomach. As he ran, he glanced over his shoulder, and saw the procession pass by. Still walking on, oblivious to his presence, or just uncaring that he was there.

He then could not hold the vomit in anymore, as it rushed up his windpipe, and projected onto the dirt beneath him.

Jacoby shivered as the lurching in his stomach soon stopped, and stared through the trees at the people passing by on the road. He could not believe the amount of people there, walking in a daze with Bella. It had to be at least half the town, he thought in shock.

As he made his way to the edge of the town, just behind the fishing port, Jacoby breathed easier as he saw that the procession was now gone, far up the track leading out of the town behind him. He could not count himself safe though, as he silently paced across the stone square as light-footed as he could, keeping his senses sharp, aware that he may not be out of this surreal danger.

The sounds in the town now seemed almost hollow, like it was built on a Hollywood sound stage, as every small noise seemed to be amplified.

Each step he took seemed so much louder than it should be. The air itself seemed to be watching him.

Passing the port office, with St Jude's spire now visible over the building ahead, Jacoby let his guard down for one, brief moment.

As he did, an arm reached out and grabbed him by the sleeve, wrenching him to the side. His yelp was soon silenced by a stern voice.

"Shhhhhh!" Anna Ólafsdóttir hissed under her breath and she dragged Jacoby down into the shadow of the port office building. "You gotta be quiet," she added in a harsh rasp.

Jacoby stared at the woman, wide-eyed. "What's happening, are you one of them?" he pleaded weakly.

"No time for that," Anna said as she pulled the priest back with her into the darkness of the office.

The HMS Dreadnought moved slowly and silently through the deepest waters of the Atlantic Ocean.

In this submersible's control room, a young man sat in front of a bank of monitors and computer interfaces. In his twenties, Navigation Officer Daniel Rooke was a long way from the streets of Edinburgh that he had called home, and to him, it seemed a lifetime since he was last there. Even though it had only been a few months since he joined this crew, he found that time passed much slower on a submarine, and he felt like he had been trapped in this metal cylinder for years.

Deep in a daydream about sitting in his local pub with friends, a pint of IPA in his hand, and rugby on the TV, he did not immediately notice the proximity alarm light start to flicker at him from his console.

The red flashing light started its blinking a few moments before the warning tone in his headphones sounded, ripping him out of his homesick thoughts, with its whining wail.

As the alarm caught his attention, he noticed on his port video feed, a large object fill the screen as it came toward the submarine, head-on.

That video feed image was normally dark, with only a dozen feet of illumination from the subs light, and nothing but the darkness of the depths ahead, but now it lit up with the gray of an object that eclipsed the screen as it collided with them. He had no time to think before the whole vessel shuddered.

Instinctively, Adam leaned forward and hit the red button on his panel, one which sounded the siren throughout the vessel. Not that anyone didn't know something was wrong already, what with the violent thud that had just tilted them to the side.

"Full stop!" Came the call from the head of the watch, from his position at the back of the control room.

After a few moments, with the siren ringing, the submarine drifted sideways until its engines kicked in and slowed its movement down to correct its tilt.

"What the hell was that?" The captain shouted as he staggered into the control room, wiping the sleep from his eyes after this unwelcome waking. "Damage report?" He commanded to the head of the watch, who was busily checking his monitors.

"Seems okay, Captain," the man replied loudly, trying to make his voice clearly heard over the continuing siren. "No breaches I can see."

"Rooke, what the hell was it?" The Captain barked as he moved over to navigation. "And someone please, turn that bloody racket off!"

Quickly, the siren was silenced as the Captain leaned in over Daniel's shoulder.

"I can assume as we're still here, it wasn't a missile?" The Captain asked sarcastically, his tone laced with a restrained anger.

"N-no sir," Adam stuttered as he stared at various monitors. "It came out of nowhere. Sensors didn't trip either."

"Could be debris from above?" The Captain said as he turned back to his first officer, who was now letting fear get the better of him. "Turn on all the lamps," he ordered.

The first officer almost panicked as he protested, "That will give our position away, won't it, Captain?."

"I'm quite aware of that, but there's no damage, so it's not an enemy attack."

As full beams of light from all sides of the

submarine suddenly illuminated their brightest. The hidden black depths were immediately exposed. The extreme brilliance of these lights all over the vessel shone brightly through the darkness and silhouetted a horror they could not fathom.

As the captain stared at the multiple monitors, at the seas around them, he was at a loss for words. Floating in vast numbers were creatures of the sea. All of them dead. All listing hopelessly in all directions around them. From fish to whales, the lights exposed the outlines of hundreds and thousands of floating carcasses.

Before the Captain could say anything, a strong pain shot through his mind, as it did the entire crews. A communal severe migraine.

This doomed submarine had no idea of the creature that now lurked below them, walking along the bottom of the ocean. Bloated from the sea waters invading her being, Petra continued on her journey. Where she went, as she traversed the deep and unforgiving ocean, all that was living fell under her spell, and all that was caught in her proximity, soon died. Whether fish or mammal all were cursed. All had no hope of escape.

At fourteen, Anna Ólafsdóttir was sick of being babysat by a never-ending procession of different members of the township, all because her father wanted to be out on the seas, instead of spending his time raising her as he should do. Her father had missed every birthday and most Christmases since she could remember. All because *'Fish don't have holidays'*, *'The sea feeds and clothes you'*, or her personal favorite, *'You are too young to understand.'* She would have understood, but none of the other fishermen's children suffered the same neglect. And it was not only her that felt this. Most of the people who looked after her when her father was away only did so out of pity. A pity she hated to see in their eyes. All of them did that, except one, and that one was the person who soon took over as her primary babysitter, when the town's pity turned to resentment, as Ólaf had used all of their goodwill asking for favors; Emmet Jones, the Lighthouse Keeper.

For the past year, Anna had spent more time perched on the edge of the lighthouse main gallery, her legs dangling through its metal bars, overlooking the seas below. In all weathers, she loved to sit there and stare outward. Whether watching the other kids from the town foolishly swim around to the bluffs to explore the caves within—a very dangerous pastime that they all seemed to do as a rite of passage—Or seeing the trawlers come back on the summer sunset, a truly beautiful sight to behold, as dozens of them all floated back under a reddish, dreamlike sky.

Anna loved this spot more than any other in the town, and Emmet was more than happy for her company, as he regularly sat beside her, sharing her love of the sea as they stared in silence, no matter the weather. Comfortable in each other's company enough to not have to talk to fill the silence.

Emmet Jones Jr. was never a man of words, not anymore anyway. Not since the accident that changed his world so many years ago. Though Anna never asked him about what happened, the large scar that ran over his balding pate detailed extensive damage.

The people in the town often spoke in whispers that, as a young boy, Emmet lived in the same lighthouse with his father, Emmet Sr, who was then the lighthouse keeper. Young Emmet followed his father around all the time. Doting on him. At school, Emmet only ever talked about two things: the lighthouse and his father. They were his world, and his father returned that love. A closer father and son unit than most others, his father taught him all about the lighthouse, every nook and cranny. And together they happily ran it. By age ten, Emmet could have easily run the entire place on his own. He could work the lantern, he knew all the radio call signs, and he could even remove and install the fresnel lens. And for this, his father could not have been more proud of his son.

But like all things in life, nothing is forever, and tragedy is often just around the corner, skulking.

Their time together in their idyllic life ended when a gale blew into Port Gaynor. A violent wind that showed no mercy on all it collided with. And on one dark evening during, when the lighthouse beamed brightly to warn all ships away, Emmet Sr had lost his footing on the main gallery, as the pervasive wind battered against him. Unable to grab onto the railing tight enough, he had slipped backward, and fallen over the railing, pushed by the storm. His body tumbled through the gale and smashed onto the ground below. He did not fall alone, though. As the wind had pushed Emmet Sr. back, his assistant, his son, had reached out and grabbed hold of his father's leg. He tried with all of his might to weigh them both down against the bluster, but nature had proved too strong, as it ripped them both off the walkway and down to their collective doom.

Tumbling through the night, Emmet had soon lost grip of his father, and as though spared by the very storm that caused their fall, he had been blown further outward due to his slight frame and light weight. With his father catching the jagged outcrop of rocks at the edge of the bluffs at the base of the lighthouse, Emmet Jr's small body missed these, and he instead fell down the cliff side and into the deep water.

He was not spared injury, though. The next day, after the storm had passed, when one of the fishing boats found Emmet Jr floating along. He was unconscious and had a large, deep gouge across his head. Somehow, even with his brains visible through the wound, this boy still breathed.

After many operations to fix his broken bones and to repair his skull, the doctor's prognosis was dire. They had to remove a large portion of his brain, as the damage to it was so severe, and with all their experience, they could not see how this boy would survive beyond a few days.

He had proved them all wrong though. He had pulled through, but who came out the other side was a quiet, sad person. One who only remembered the lighthouse. He remembered everything about what he was taught by his now dead father, but could not remember that night. He could not remember most things. He could speak, though with a long slur. But the townsfolk did not have the patience to listen to him, as they took his labored speech to label him dumb. Which he may have been by their terms, but he knew more about the lighthouse than anyone else.

After years in care, Emmet Jr walked out of the home on his own steam as a twenty-six-year-old. Though he had with what doctors callously called a 'child's mind in a man's body'.

For years he did nothing except wander around the town, talking to anyone who would listen about the lighthouse, which was now being managed by a new keeper. Emmet became a bit of a joke. *The Lighthouse Man*, as he was dubbed, became a figure of ridicule for the adults, as well as the children.

A few years later, after the lighthouse manager's position became available, fortune would soon smile on Emmet Jones Jr. Though being told otherwise by the gossiping townsfolk, the local coast guard manager had felt pity for Emmet.

Having appointed his father to the position many years before, he remembered vividly, the young Emmet being a wunderkind with the operation of the lighthouse. He had witnessed the boy doing jobs that only adults should have been capable of.

Whether a lapse in common sense or just stupidity—as some inferred—the coast guard manager gave Emmet Jr a trial run as the new keeper; mainly to see if the now mentally impaired man could still do the job, his father once did. All doubts were proven wrong though, as Emmet excelled and was eventually handed the full-time position.

As a keeper, Emmet was always a solitary man, but still loved being around people when he could. They just did not like being around him, as they did not know how to speak to him. Anna Ólafsdóttir was different. She did not judge, nor get annoyed with him if it took him a long time to say a few simple words. And just because of that, he was more than happy to have her stay with him when her father was out fishing, as was she. In fact, she sometimes encouraged her father to take extra jobs, just so she could stay at the lighthouse with Emmet.

As Anna grew, her contact with Emmet remained. Even when she got the job as Port Manager, they remained close. Beyond her now professional link to the lighthouse, she would cook him dinner a couple of times a week, and the two would have constant radio conversations as they each sat in their work offices, whiling away the hours. Port Gaynor was not a busy port after all, so most days were filled with them playing a silly game of I Spy, something stupid, as neither of them could see what the other one could see.

Anna saw Emmet as her only real friend. Her only friend by choice, and the feeling was most definitely mutual. Separated by nearly four decades in age, they were like brother and sister. He looked after her when she was young. Now she was older, she would do the same for him in his advancing years.

Sarah Babbidge was dead, at least what she was no more.

As her eyes opened, she felt a cold. A comforting cold.

She then remembered the knife slicing her throat.

She remembered as her blood jetted in torrents into the stone bowl, the undead priest praising his god.

She then knew nothing.

At least nothing for a few seconds of her death. For when her death awoke, she found herself lying on the altar in the Old Chapel.

"Praise Dagon!" The undead Father Harris decreed as he stood above her, looking out to the congregation.

Slowly turning her head to one side, Sarah then

saw the gathered masses who cheered in reply to the decree.

At the front of the altar was the large stone bowl, stained with blood, yet empty.

Only a few moments before, all the people here had taken turns, one by one, by dipping their fingers into the bowl of Sarah's crimson lifeblood, then wiped those fingers over their tongues, all in a macabre communion. When each had done this, they returned to their place in the chapel. And throughout all of this, each and every person had the same listless expression on their face.

As Sarah's gaze drifted lazily to Father Harris standing above her, she saw his milky eyes, and she grinned.

"Welcome, my child," Harris said in a low cracked voice.

Sarah Babbige, how she once was, would have screamed in horror and fought against what she would have seen as a perversion. But that Sarah Babbidge was dead. Now, she was something different. And an ancient knowledge began unleashing itself deep inside of her.

What once was her purpose was now nothing of consequence.

All there was within her mind was her new purpose.

She knew what she had to do.

She did not mourn her old life.

She did not fear that she was dead.

She did not wonder about where she found herself.

She just felt love. Her new god's grace.

"Welcome," Father Harris said to her. "You have much to do."

"Praise Dagon," Sarah said with a smile, her voice now a gargled version of what it once was.

Eleven

Michael walked through the woodlands that stood between the hospital and the town. At his side, projected within his mind, Petra walked too.

Everything seemed peaceful here.

"I can feel your desire to ask me something," Petra smirked. "Why don't you just ask?"

"What do you want?" he said. "You showed me those things in my mind. What was it? What was any of it?"

"My father?" she replied. "He is the harbinger of renewal. And it is time for this existence to be wiped away."

"Time? Why?"

"Why does there have to be a reason? It is just time. Everything is cyclical, and happens when it happens, again and again, through reality, existence and sanity."

Michael stopped in his tracks, trying to figure

out what he was being told. "How can any of that be true? If any of it was meant to be, then it would just happen. It wouldn't need me, or you, or anyone else."

Petra smiled, "I guess I can't fool you, can I?"

"Was anything you showed me real?"

"Does it matter?" She started to skip as she talked. If it was not for her open eye sockets, bleeding wounds, and cruel smile, it may have looked like an innocent moment. But as she was, her skipping along seemed malevolent. "All that should matter to you is two things. The first is that I live up to my end of the bargain. The second is that you please me enough that I don't ever do this again."

"Do what again?" Michael said, and almost immediately regretted it.

Petra quickly shot him an empty glance, and as soon as she did so, a wracking pain in his body flooded his nerves. Causing each to feel like they were on fire again.

Collapsing to the dirt ground in a fit of pained screams, Petra waved her hands in the air. As she did so, the sky turned a deep red, and from above, things started to fall around the wooded area. Hitting the ground with a thud. A rainstorm of dead birds.

"Please," Michael wheezed, trying to catch his breath, imploring his vicious childlike companion. "Please stop."

As a victorious smile crept on her face yet again,

the sky quickly lost its red hue. The birds all stopped falling, and Michael's pain subsided.

He was quickly back to how he was.

Just as he was about to stand, Petra kneeled in front of him.

"I can make your world whatever I want it to be," she said. "I need you to know what I can do. Not as a threat, but so you realize that I am serious, and will stop at nothing. Your pain does not hurt me, despite me being in you, and I can hold you from death forever."

"Why don't you just control me, then?" Michael asked. "You controlled the doctor and the others, right? You can control how I feel. Why not just make me help you? Why ask me at all? Why not just take over?"

"Please," Petra's smile dropped. "I said I did not know what happened to them. Did I cause it? Maybe. But not through intent. And why would you want me to control you? Do you want to lose yourself?"

Michael stared at her for a moment in silence, trying to accept her words.

"Can you even control me?" he asked, dreading the reaction.

Instead of showing anger, Petra turned and began to walk away from him. Leading the walk toward town.

For a few moments, Michael looked around at the surrounding woodland. He breathed deeply catching his breath.

"Are you coming?" She called out loudly.

Before he could take a step in her direction, from out of the deep recesses of his mind, Michael heard something. Something from the darkest shadows inside.

I'm so scared, a small girl's voice cried out in his mind. *Please help me go home, Father*. This voice was heard as if whispered, then caught on the breeze as it drifted by his ear. It was Petra, the innocent uncorrupted Petra.

"I've called every port I could," Anna said quietly, motioning to the large radio transmitter that sat in the Port Office. "Even called out to ships. Nothing. Nada. Can't call up anyone. All messages I send out, only dead air comes back. Been like that for two hours now."

Both she and Jacoby were sat on the wooden floor, directly underneath the office window, hiding out of view from anyone who might pass.

"Two hours?" Jacoby asked, his volume matching Anna's. "Was I up there that long?"

"Where?"

"The Old Chapel."

Anna shrugged, then sounded mournful as she spoke. "About then I heard the screams. Heard the Aldertons. Bobbi and Andy were screaming at their grandpa, Henry. Shoutin' for him to stop. I didn't know what it was they were talkin' about. But they were just at the bait and tackle shop across the street. They shouted and shouted... 'Stop! Please, grandpa!" Anna's voice mimicked a small child's before it quickly returned to its normal tone. "I got up. Walked out to see what the fuss was. But just as I did. I saw it happen. Henry was walking across the street. His face was totally blank. Like a sheet. As if he'd seen a ghost. Totally not hearing Bobbi cryin' or Andy screamin'. But Andy didn't let up, just like never did. He ran up right behind his gramps, and grabbed him by the arm, yanking him around." Her gaze drifted from Jacoby and down to her feet. She took a deep and mentally painful breath into her lungs.

"What happened?" Jacoby asked. "Was Henry like the others that just walked up to the bluffs?"

Anna nodded regretfully. "It all seemed kinda normal. But just as Andy's hand grabbed onto Henry's arm." she paused for a second as if replaying the image over in her head. "Just as he made any contact. Henry's face changed to one of... It wasn't right. He just smiled. Just like that. A huge grin turned on. And he turned round and started beatin' on Andy, really batterin' him. Like all of a sudden. Like a silverback does. Little Bobbi screamed so hard. But before I could get to them, to stop Henry. Out of the store, Debbie Benson walked by. If you know her? Woman who runs the Cinema. Her face was just like Henry's. All blank. Then, as she passed by Henry beatin' on Andy, he suddenly stopped and stood up next to her. Both of them then just turned and began walkin' slowly back up the bluffs. They walked in time. And both like nothin' happened. I stood back and let them pass. Neither even shared a glance with me for a second. Like they didn't register anything. Or care to. I then went over, but Andy. He was gone. Henry had beaten the life out of the poor child. Bobbi was still there inconsolable. And that teacher, Aiden Grey then ran over. It was so stupid, but he was dressed as a wizard. I still don't know why, but I kinda laughed at it. Probably for a party or something. But there I was, seein' this poor kid get killed by his own kin, and there I am, chucklin' inside at Will in fancy dress." she shook her head as she continued. "He took that sparkly cape off, the one that had moons 'n' shit over it, threw it over Andy's body, coverin' him up from Bobbi like, then ran over to her and held her tight as she cried into him. Then... Then they *all* started comin'."

Jacoby shifted his position, so he could peer over the window ledge toward the Bait shop. The covered body of the boy still lay on the sidewalk. The cape still lying over him like a mortician's sheet. Around the body, the rest of the street was barren. The doors to shops left half open. The dead boy was forgotten about, as was the town.

"I haven't been brave enough to move him yet," Anna sadly mused. "They could still be out there. The only reason I knew you weren't one of them was cos you look scared shitless. As anyone *should* be. But none of them are like that."

Jacoby turned back to her and sat back down below the window. "This can't be happening," He said in a weak and tearful voice. His emotions swelled inside of him. Starting to push through any brave exterior. "What do you think it is? Gas leak? A virus?"

Anna smiled a pained smile. "I can't explain it, and I sure as shit can't say what you saw. A dead priest talkin' you said?"

Jacoby had neglected to tell her about not being able to save Sarah, and more importantly about what he saw in the procession; her father walking, looking freshly dead, yet as undead as Father Harris. He had wanted to tell Anna. He wanted to be the voice of calm and reason. But he couldn't. And for the second time today, he felt like a failure in the eyes of his god, for he saw it as his own cowardice manifest yet again, even if he saw his omission as a kindness.

"After Debbie and Henry left," Anna continued. "Everyone then started coming out of the shops. Houses. Down the street. From all corners. All just starin' forward. All just walkin' the same way up to the bluffs." She paused for a moment and rubbed the bridge of her nose, then sighed as she tried to push on with the words. "After there were more shouts. So many more. And just like that poor kid lying cold out there, the shouts, then they turned to screams, then to begging cries, then... Then... to nothin'."

"Do you think this could be the end times?"

Jacoby asked as he tried to solve the puzzle of what he and Anna had seen.

Anna leaned forward. "Is any of this in your Bible? Zombies? Mind control?"

Jacoby pondered for a moment as he took a breath, "For the Lord himself, with a cry of command, with the archangel's call and with the sound of god's trumpet, will descend from heaven, and the dead in Christ will rise first. Then we who are alive, who are left, will be caught up in the clouds together with them to meet the Lord in the air; and so we will be with the Lord forever." He looked at Anna almost apologetically. "So, yeah. It's kinda in the Bible."

Anna sighed. "Well, in any case, I gotta go get Emmet from the lighthouse. He ain't answering my calls. You're more than welcome to join me if you want?"

"You wanna go up there? That's where those people are," Jacoby protested. "He could be one of them. We should run. Now." Before Anna could reply, the priest hurriedly added, "There's got to be people like us here. In town. Hiding out. That can't have been the whole town walking there. Like, where did the teacher take the young girl?"

"They ran up the street." Anna shrugged as she pointed behind her. "Dunno where though."

"Up that street? Toward St Jude's?" Jacoby asked.

"I got no idea," Anna replied. "Look, I gotta go find Emmet. He wasn't one of them last time. He's gonna have answers. He saw something like this a while ago. He used to tell me stuff about it. I thought it was just some fun. But it's exactly what's goin' on."

"What d'you mean?"

1982

"The clouds came in from the water," Emmet said in his usual slow and slurred voice. His delivery was pained and tested the patience of most of the townsfolk. But not Anna. She found the way he talked calming. Without the urgency of all other adults. Though sometimes *what* he told her, the stories he would recant, would make the young girl worry that any adult would put him away if they heard them, for being crazy.

"The clouds came all over here. And everyone fell asleep."

With the dull orange glow of the lighthouse office lamp lending an almost dreamlike atmosphere to the room, Emmet's words sounded more like a fairytale, as opposed to him answering a question about what scared him the most.

"I didn't sleep like them," he continued. "I was here. I looked out the window. Then there was a horrible sound. Kind same as a lion. The sea was red and boiling like a kettle. I ran to town. Walked around. *'Wake up'*. I shouted that to the people asleep. All over the road. By the boats. All lying down. *'Wake up'*. I kept shouting and shouting.

Nothing. They stayed asleep. I walked around. Then... Then they all stood. I tried to speak. No. They didn't see me. They just walked to the church by the sea. Then the clouds went away. Then people came from the other side of town. They asked what happened. I didn't know. I said what I saw. They laughed at me. I told them about the monster I heard. They laughed again. Then, everything went back to normal." As he told his story, he became confused, still unsure of what happened. "Then those people came back. Didn't know what I was saying. But the scary part is. Later on. Lots of people just went. Gone. Never seen again. No one asked why. No one cared. I was the only one caring."

"And that's what you're most scared of?" Anna asked. Not understanding the point to the story.

Emmet nodded. "It *was* scary. Very scary."

Anna smiled. He had told this strange and incoherent story before. But she would never tell him that. She was just happy to be here, and happy to talk.

"Well, I'm afraid of spiders," she said, changing the subject away from his strange tale.

Emmet smiled, though as he told the story, he felt the same fear that he had felt on that day.

Twelve

Anna glanced over her shoulder at the priest, who hurriedly walked in the opposite direction. Jacoby had told her that he had to go back to his church. He had to help those in need. He said he would come find her as soon as he could—But she had heard lies like that her whole life. The same lies from people who said what others wanted to hear. She had heard her father enough times tell her that he would be home in time for tea. That he would be at her party. That he would be taking her to hockey practice. That he would teach her how to drive. That he would repay the money he had borrowed. But each time, she had seen that same forlorn expression that was on Jacoby's face, on her father's. She knew he was going to run away, and she could not blame him. She wanted to run too, she just knew she could not abandon her friend.

Her concern then turned to Emmet. It was

unlike him to not answer his radio, but even if he was standing alongside the others in the mindless horde, she had to find out the truth. She could not run away like the priest had, not without Emmet in tow.

In her panic, as she crept along the edges of the street, up to the path to the bluffs, she tried as hard as she could to not think of her father. She couldn't face what she had seen out of the port window. The priest may have hidden seeing the undead Ólaf Hansson from her, but it was in fact a moot point. He didn't *have* to tell her. She had seen Ólaf for herself, marching amongst the masses, half of his face missing. A living impossibility with parts of his skull now bloodily exposed. A wound that she knew was so bad that it left no chance of survival. She pushed all those thoughts of shock as far away as she could. She had already wept silently in the port office. But she could not afford grief or upset at the moment. Not until she and Emmet were safe, and this was all over. She would have to grieve another day.

As Jacoby approached St Jude's, he could hear a sobbing coming from a nearby alley. As he passed by, he caught a glimpse of a shadowed figure in anguish. He could not tell who it was, and he could have done the Christian thing and stopped to help them—as his conscience told him to do—But whoever they were, they were now on their own.

He was getting out of here. He was running away. His god had abandoned this town, so he would abandon it too. His intent was to grab a bag of essentials from the rectory, then run as far as he could away from this town.

"We are going back there," Petra said as she skipped happily alongside Michael. Though she existed within Michael's brain and not in reality, he almost felt she was flesh and blood, right next to him. Despite her eyeless, hideous appearance, he even had flashes of considering her a young girl, as opposed to an ancient monstrous possessor.

"What is there?" He replied.

"My death," she said in a sing-song tone. "My offering to my father. I will get sucked out of your mind and then..." A flash of confusion traced across her face. "I'm not sure. They will be waiting for me, though. Even without my chosen body."

Michael stopped in his tracks and chuckled. "You don't know what you're doing? How do you know all of this?"

Petra's footsteps came to a stop, and for a few moments, she paused in silence.

In a blink of an eye, she whirled around to Michael, launched herself at him, and knocked him to the ground.

"You dare mock me?" she seethed. Even as an apparition from inside his mind, she could hurt him badly. "You forget your place. You forget what I am. You forget *who* I am."

Michael looked confused, as Petra smiled, and her next words came out lascivious and twisted, "Oh yes, I never did tell you who I am." As she leaned in closer, blood dripped from her eye sockets. "I am Baal, the corrupted. I am the child of Dagon. Bringer of the end... I am what you fear. I am doubt. I am hate. I am pain. I am the devil in the details of this world's last breath. And you will show me respect!"

With a sudden smile, she continued. "Anyway, in answer to your question," she happily said as Michael clambered to his feet, bedraggled and struggling to breathe after her attack. "I have no idea what awaits me. You destroyed my body and trapped me. This was not part of what should be. Your plan broke our prophecy."

"I never *planned* this," he croaked.

Her head tilted to the side as she faced him. "No?"

"I wanted to save her. The real girl. Petra." He said. "But you broke free, and... You didn't wake up after the bullet hit. You were unconscious. They came to take you away. To keep you locked up."

"The body is still alive?" Petra asked, astounded. "How did I not know this? I see your thoughts. I see them *all*."

"All I know is this was an accident. I had *no idea* you escaped. I thought you were still in that body. They wouldn't have taken you if they knew the exorcism worked!"

"Who are *they*?" Petra asked.

Michael did not reply. He did not have to.

"The Vatican?" She guessed. "They have my chosen vessel?"

He weakly nodded in confirmation.

"Whatever, something has now changed." She turned. "Or I'd still be in slumber, and the air would not carry the sweet stench of death."

When Albert Gutierrez won the Democratic nomination to be the commander and chief of the United States of America, he never dreamed that the public would have voted for him as they did. Now as he sat in the presidential war room, alongside the heads of all of his country's departments, from military to communications, he stared at images being shown to him on the large screen. Mounted on the wall beside the large round table they now sat at, the screen displayed images of the recent tragedy. Images of death. Thousands of bodies lining the streets from the square out from the Vatican, then eastward. Town after town, each looked the same as the last, with people fallen, each were lifeless, yet with a look of contentment on their faces. Italian, then French, united in this unimaginable disaster.

"We have relative certainty that it originated in

Rome," General Stanley said in his booming voice. Looking more walrus than man, and an overgrown mustache on his round face, Stanley hid any confusion that he may have felt in what he was presenting with a strong, military exterior. "Then it seems to have gone off the coast, reemerged at Narbonne, France. Then along to Bayonne, where it went into the Atlantic. All of this was in a day. Now that's hundreds and hundreds of miles, even as the crow flies. So, whatever it was, has considerable speed. That's *if* it's above ground."

"If?" President Gutierrez asked. "What do you mean?"

Stanley turned and looked directly at his leader. "Mr. President," he said mournfully. "We have no witnesses who are alive. All CCTV is fried, picking up nothing from these violent events. Not even a satellite recorded a thing. Now it's logical to assume chemical attacks—if this was one—maybe would have hit two cities, but this is across the map in a straight line." Turning to his left, he motioned to a woman who sat nervously beside him. A woman who was obviously intimidated by where she was and who she was in the presence of. "This is Doctor Ingrid Hoff," Stanley said. "Head of earth sciences at Harvard. I reached out to her earlier to get answers, as this wasn't adding up as some kind of attack." Stanley then nodded to her. "Doctor Hoff, please, can you tell them what you told me?"

Sitting back down in his seat, Stanley then turned to the president and nodded.

After a few moments of the room waiting on her, Doctor Hoff felt too nervous about being in such company, she fought to speak.

President Gutierrez cut in. "Please, Doctor Hoff. I know it's intimidating, but we're all in the same boat." He spoke in a comforting tone. "I thought that today was going to be another day dealing with inflation, so trust me when I say we're all on unfamiliar ground."

"M-Mr. President," Doctor Hoff began with a stutter. "When General Stanley contacted me, I looked at all the data I could get from over the last 48 hrs, from as many departments at the university as I could, as well as observatories, my contacts at NASA, even paleontologists."

Albert turned to his assistant with a quizzical eyebrow.

"Dinosaurs," the assistant whispered.

"And we can say there were no meteorological events to speak of," Hoff continued. "No solar flares. No seismic anomalies. Literally, nothing in the sciences that I could find could explain what was happening. Now my first thought was going to be a solar storm, as they can affect—"

"Dr. Hoff," Albert interrupted. "Please only keep on the subject. We haven't got time to discuss what we thought it could be."

"Sorry, Mr. President," she replied, losing her train of thought.

"That's ok," he smiled. "You were saying that science didn't explain it?"

"Yes!" she exclaimed. "But there *is* historical precedent to at least some of it."

"This happened before?" Albert asked, taken aback. "When?"

"We have records of anomalous events where scores of people fell down dead, about 3 in total. The last one on record was in 1952 and that was in Winchester, England."

"England," Albert exclaimed, visibly shocked.

"Now we only have written records of this, from diary entries, etcetera, so nothing is 100% fact and should be treated with some skeptical caution." Taking out a piece of paper from her inside pocket, Dr. Hoff unfolded it and read aloud. "From the diary of Padre Martain, who was a Vatican scribe. 'Then the people of Venta Belgarum saw a great dark cloud escape the house of the possessed. Each soul the cloud touched was also touched by the very devil that dwelled within. Their souls numbered in their dozens. And soon all surrounded the building. The dark cloud continued to grow and contaminate. Yet when the expulsion was completed, the clouds disappeared to the heavens—'"

"Are we really listening to this?" Albert exclaimed. "No offense, Doctor Hoff, but this is all religion."

"Please Mr. President," General Stanley spoke up. "I'm the same as you, and can't fathom this being about hoodoo, but let her finish."

With a look of relenting annoyance, Albert

raised his hand up to Doctor Hoff, signaling her to continue.

"I..." she looked down at the paper in her hand. "He said, 'when the cloud left, and the possessor was vanquished. Those corrupted by the dark cloud fell. Smiles adorning their faces. They were dead. During the event, we tried to photograph and film the proceedings as much as we could, but all films were blank when they were developed. As if nothing was ever there.'" She then put the page down and looked at the president. "Now I am a woman of science. I'm an atheist. I do not believe in gods or demons, but I know that those who do, when they see things they cannot explain, they assign their own theology as a benchmark. Here, some priests thought they were exorcizing a demon, and they were assigned to by the Vatican. The scribe's words I read are kind of official account."

"So?" Albert asked, not seeing her point.

"So, strip out god from the equation. They say there was a cloud that made people change in some way. Then when it went, they died with a smile. Here we have towns where lots of people have died with that same look on their face. And the last radio communication we managed to intercept from a policeman in Bayonne was, and this is a translation, from a call into his station. 'I'm just outside Langon, by the LaRue farm. There's a dark cloud over the fields. It looks really weird. Like smoke, but it's moving like it's alive. It's.... Oh god... Help...' and that's where it cut off. Next time this policeman was seen, was in the photos from the beach at Bayonne. Floating among the hundreds of other unfortunates."

The president looked shocked.

"Now I know this is not an answer," she said. "But this kind of event has happened before. And each time, just as quick as it came, it went."

"Thank you Doctor Hoff," General Stanley said as he motioned to her to sit. He then turned to the president. "And that's the best explanation we have. But now, unlike any time it's been spoken of before, *now* it's moving. We have no explanation as to why that is. But we can only hope it stops before it reaches our shores."

"How many vessels have we lost contact with?" The president asked.

"Two. The Brit's lost a sub and we can't contact a carrier. As far as we can tell, anything crossing near the straight line it travels has died." He turned to an engineer at a computer terminal. "Show them," he requested in a hushed tone.

On the screen, the image changed to one showing a map of the world and a line going from Rome across the south of France, then across the Atlantic in a straight line.

"That's the route it's going?" Albert asked.

The general nodded in reply. "Next picture," he said to the engineer.

The screen changed to an image of the sea with scores of animals dead and floating in usually dark water.

"This was taken by a French Coast Guard helicopter examining the scene." The general walked over to the image and pointed to the darkness of the water. "You can see here that there is something in the water. At least coloring the water, which we can assume is what killed the wildlife. And the Brit's sub was 150 miles off the coast, here," he pointed to a marker on the red line. "And the carrier lost contact here." He then moved his finger to a second marker on the red line, nearer to America. "The helicopter that took this, crashed into the ocean less than 10 minutes after it made an initial low pass. One where they mentioned that a black smoke was coming out of the water."

Albert wished that this was a nightmare that he could wake up from. "Do we know how far it's reached?" He asked, dreading the answer.

"We have some planes out, keeping their distance, but using long range equipment to monitor the dead fish that keep rising to the surface along the line. The latest data places it 600 miles off the American coast, and it's picking up speed."

Albert sighed.

"If it continues the straight line, it will make land at a town called Port Gaynor." General Stanley concluded. "A fishing village on the south of the Eastern seaboard."

"What can we do?"

"I've spoken to my counterparts in the UK, France and Italy, as well as NATO," Stanley replied. "The only answer is... Nothing. We have nothing to fight. Nothing we can bomb. No idea if it's above or below ground. It could be a moving submersible releasing toxins, or something coming from inside the earth, like an ecological event that's following a new fault line. We can only wait to see. I got a platoon headed to that town now, and they'll quarantine as much as they can to try to halt any possible incursion. That's *if* that is what this is, not that there is any evidence of that fact. We just have to accept that until we know more, we can only contain. We can't react until we have more intel."

"And by then it will be too late," the president said, as he felt a coldness unlike anything he had ever felt. It was as if his stomach was filling with ice. "We can't even warn people, can we? In case we cause a panic."

THIRTEEN

The night felt oppressive as darkness enveloped the path from the base of the port, up to the bluffs higher up where the Old Chapel stood. Without any streetlights, the path was only illuminated by the moon that kept hiding behind the dark clouds, the clouds that still threatened to erupt just as they had done over the past few days. This town seemed entrenched within the eye of the storm that brought the torrents of icy rain and hurricane winds, as in the far distance the wind and rain howled, waiting to return. Being in the middle of a violent storm for so long was felt somehow unnatural, as the calm should never last that long.

Anna ran up the path, hugging the shadows along the tree-line as she moved, wide-eyed and on the lookout for any danger. On the opposite side of the path to her, a small fence was the only thing between her and an increasingly steep cliff face. Ahead, just over the hill a dozen feet ahead stood the Old Chapel, then further on, at the apex of the bluffs, her destination lay in wait; the Port Gaynor lighthouse.

She could see from where she was that the lighthouse lamp was dark. And this was the first time the lamp had been dark, for as long as she could remember. At night, its beam would shine out over the dark expanse of the Atlantic, a beam that all the town could see from each vantage point along the coast. Tonight, though, the Atlantic remained in shadow, as did any boats, that each would have no spinning light to warn them away.

Despite not being obese, Anna was not thin, she was not fit at all, as her diet and penchant for whiskey meant that her sprint to find Emmet was not an easy one. She wheezed the cold night air into her lungs, though did not let any pains in her body overtake her caution. Though she had no idea what was the cause to what was happening, she knew enough to know that the people that trod this path earlier, were dangerous. She had witnessed as much outside the bait shop.

She had also witnessed... Her father.

As much as she tried to push the thoughts away, to exorcise her emotions down until she could afford to address them in her own time, the grief approached like her like a sudden sledgehammer to the brain, as without warning images of Ólaf's destroyed undead face slammed into her.

Just after she had witnessed the boy being murdered outside the bait shop, Anna was about to run for help as Henry and Debbie walked away in a daze, but as she peered out of her office door, her father approached from the junction at the end of the road, causing her to lock herself away in the office in terror. As Ólaf passed, Anna had been brave enough to get a full view of the gored out right side of her father's face as he passed the window. Hollow and bloody, with bone and brain on full display, but yet, he still walked. She would have ignored the violence evident on his face and ran out crying to see him, but she had quickly seen the town's doctor following close behind. The man had two knives embedded deep within his brain, as he too walked impossibly under his own steam.

Anna was normally a rational woman, one who was never beholden to flights of fancy. Never one to tell a tall tale. Never a believer in conspiracy theories. Never a follower of religion. But on whom she also knew were not intelligent enough to know the impossible, and without scientists and experts there to logically explain events, they would all seem supernatural and terrifying. Thunder and lightning being a prime example. Without science there to explain them, anyone would logically assume that a god would be showing their anger in the sky. But now, with this, she could not explain the logic or reality of her father and the doctor's conditions. She could only think of the word; zombies. Beyond the films and books showing the brain-eating monsters, she had no other word for what she saw. They were dead, they were violent. They were seemingly vacant of personality. What else were they if not zombies?

When these images and thoughts ran through her mind, Anna cautiously hurried up the path, her breath pained and short as the grief suddenly hit her again. Hitting her hard.

She could not control her torrent of emotion, as she fell to the stony path in a flood of anguished tears. Fighting back for as long as she could, the emotions that she had kept bottled up for too long now. Now it all exploded in a loud wail.

Emmet peered out of the lighthouse window at the chapel down the bluffs. He had seen the long procession of townsfolk lead there and walk inside into the dilapidated church building.

Through his binoculars, he had seen what he hoped that he would never see again, not since that day in 75 when a low dark cloud covered the town and caused the people to act strange. A cloud that he too breathed, yet felt no effects from.

He now sensed a horrific déjà vu as he watched the people below, the same people affected before, act in the same way again as each other. He had witnessed some of them change back to normal after the first time, but had presumed it was now all done with. He looked at folks below intently, like they were all ants walking in unison with no mind of their own.

Back in 1975 when it first happened, Emmet had tried to stop one of them, but they ignored his worried question. When he stood in their way again, they had suddenly turned on him. A horrible, twisted and cruel expression caressing their face as their arms reached out to Emmet to grip his throat. He was lucky that he managed to avoid this violent action and sprint away. They had tried to run after him, but out of sheer luck, he had managed to lose them in the twisted streets of the town. After that, he knew to hide far away from them in the lighthouse, and not to venture into town again, unless it was really needed.

Now, though, he had stared through his binoculars in terrified awe at the very same people walking to the Old Chapel. Yet now some were different; he had seen the undead Ólaf near the front, staggering in, as mindless as the rest.

When he heard Anna's voice calling him on the radio, he could not bring himself to answer it, not knowing that her father was... was... He did not know *what* he was. He just did not know what to say. So, he had chosen to keep quiet and ignore all her calls. She was safer not being here and among the other possessed people. He had to keep it that way. He had to keep her safe.

His binoculars' gaze drifted from the now full

chapel and to the left along the town. It was quiet down there. But it was also the middle of the night, so Emmet knew, like before, the rest of the town was probably asleep. Hopefully asleep and unaware of what was happening.

Emmet had his own ideas about what this was, not that anyone would ever listen to him. No one except Anna.

His vision then immediately caught something on the horizon, something moving toward the town at great speed. A large dark shadow above the water, shadowed by the night and lack of lighthouse glare.

"No," he muttered in fear. Knowing full well that this was the same cloud he had seen hit the town before.

As the moonlight hit the roof of the Old Chapel, the broken tiles and rotten wood let through its bright beams, down onto the altar below.

The procession from the town had ended up here. Each stood in a crowd to witness as Father Harris smiled down at the altar, at the bloodless body of Sarah Babbidge, with her throat wound wide and open. Her eyes stared wide and lifelessly up to the sky as her body lay twisted on the stone table.

The crowd stared in silence, not one whisper, not one cough, just a mutual spell containing all humanity, leaving an eerie emptiness.

"And in the depths of existence, the one shall rise from a sacrificial embrace," Father Harris spoke, his words dry, cracked, and weak. "Rise... For the one truth."

As if on command, Sarah blinked and drew in a harsh breath, the oxygen partially escaping through the wound in her throat. Her eyes, though, still dead to look at, gray and colorless. The veil of death shifted as she could see again, and even though she could barely breathe, she felt an urge to speak. Her mind, once a convolution of dogmatic panic, was now clear.

Clear with a new mind, an ancient mind. All Sarah had been was still present, but now there was now a new control inside. One that was still her, yet without the shame of her life, without the fear of the unknown, without care for her or other's humanity. She now had a new cause. One which filled her dead brain with new vigor.

"Praise Dagon," she said, her voice broken and breathless. The words came from within her diseased soul. She stared up at the broken chapel roof, finding the strength to move, as Father Harris smiled and looked out to the congregation.

"And with the raising of the herald," he said as loudly as he could. "The past is reborn."

With a confident step, and keeping his milky eyes on the congregation, Father Harris then walked around the altar and down to the nave, walking into the middle of the large crowd.

As he glanced around smiling, dozens of

followers were now smiling back, all in his direction.

"Praise Dagon," he shouted.

"Praise Dagon," the crowd erupted in a reply.

In a matter of seconds, and moving all at once, the crowd then all leaned forward and grabbed any part of Father Harris that they could.

With an extreme and violent force, this undead ex-priest was suddenly wrenched in all directions by those who could grab at him.

As his body was caught in the hands of the congregation, they soon converged over his bloodless living corpse and tore it asunder. Ripping it into small dry morsels. Dry parts that were each soon bitten into, by any person who could reach them to grab their share. His body was, bit by bit, savaged by the baying throng, each who took turns in tearing more and more from this holy zombie's awaiting carcass. And as they tore, they also ate. And when one had swallowed their small part, each moved back to the outside of the crowd, letting one from behind through to take their turn. Like a pack of wolves with a polite streak, this was a macabre sight to behold, but not one to hear. For there were no screams. No bloody panic. Nothing. Just the sound of the act itself.

Sarah did not need to look at what was happening. She did not even wish to. She was not even curious. She knew exactly what had happened, not to mention why it had happened. She had a mission to uphold; Father Harris's, that was an old mission handed down to her, all in line with the ancient wisdom they both had shared.

Soon, the sounds of gnawing and shuffling abated as the congregation finished their meals, then turned back toward the altar.

With a slow and jittery movement, Sarah moved her legs from the stone and stood up to face the crowd. Her hair was now unkempt and blood-soaked. Her clothes were torn and bloody. Her skin was pale and mottled. But her smile was growing to its extreme, nevertheless.

"Children of the deep," she said. Her weak voice gradually finding a strong vigor through the large laceration in her neck. "Let us welcome the spawn. Baal. The corrupted."

"Praise Dagon," the crowd said loudly. "Praise Baal."

Taking a step into the crowd, Sarah then walked past where the bones of Father Harris now lay. Each picked clean in a matter of moments by the faithful. Like a shoal of piranhas, each left nothing on this undead man's skeleton.

The crowd quickly parted and made a path for Sarah, as she walked toward the open chapel's door, her movements stuttered and unnatural.

As she walked into the darkness, the crowd turned and followed her one by one in a silent procession, but as they did, the large, dark cloud that had approached from the sea had now made contact with Port Gaynor. Its billowing and wispy mist crawled over the town at an unnatural speed. Neither Sarah nor the congregation paid it any kind, not that they had their own minds to think with, for this cloud did not affect them.

FOURTEEN

Emmet had left the lighthouse and walked through the oncoming dark mist, as he avoided the bluffs that the townsfolk now stood on. He then veered into the same woods that Jacoby had run through, only hours before. But instead of finding just trees, he had also found heartbreak within there. At the tree-line, he had witnessed Anna suddenly scream whilst clutching her head, the pain coming on fast, leaving even quicker when it went a minute later.

Before Anna could take another step, Emmet had picked up a rock and hit her over the back of the head, with it causing her to lose consciousness and collapse on impact.

Then dragging her unconscious body back into the woods, Emmet then began to carry her toward the lighthouse, retracing his steps, out of sight of the possessed masses nearby.

With this mist still around, even unconsciousness could not keep Anna silent.

As she came to, Emmet had to hold her in a neck lock as he covered her mouth with his large, free hand.

He had almost cried looking down from the lighthouse, when he had seen that she was falling like *them*. And this scene overtook him, so much so he was so focused on her, that he did not hear the rattling of gunfire in the distance.

Jacoby had felt the pain in his head increasing as he sprinted down the street, heading out of the town of Port Gaynor. The dark sea clouds even now streaked their way up this empty road, looking for victims.

In the town, the streetlights had cast their orange glow among the oncoming, low-flying cloud, making the whole town seem incredibly cartoonish, nightmarish and unreal.

Jacoby had no car, so his only choice was to run. The fear had ripped him out of his life, and now, with a small rucksack of clothes on his back, he made his way, stumbling over his own steps as the torment seared through his brain.

Screaming at the top of his lungs, Jacoby eventually focused on the men staring at him in gas masks, and he staggered in his escape. Barely even feeling anything except for what was in his head, Jacoby's hands shot up and gripped his temples.

He did not feel the moment that his life switched over to his new, darker one.

He did not hear the cracking rattle of gunfire in front of him.

He did not feel the bullets tearing through his body.

It should have been agony, but it was instead sudden nothingness.

Two dozen soldiers dressed in gas masks and protective jumpsuits walked out of the orange-hued darkness, and with their machine guns held up, walking toward the town. Behind them, the sound of a large engine roared as a tank followed their pace.

No one stopped to move the fallen dead priest. These men had their mission, and they would continue on,

The cloud billowed its way across the town in a matter of minutes. Whirling its way through the air and under any door or window crack that it could. Those who had slumbered into a peaceful sleep would never have known what happened to them as they inhaled the corrupted mist, and as they soon turned and lost their mind. They each left their abodes and began to slowly march through the streets and up to the bluff's edge, where the rest of their kind waited. All still, staring out to sea.

Michael felt no such effects as he walked through the dark wisps that filled the path. In front of him, in his mind's eye, Petra skipped along.

Leading the way. Not allowing him to breathe anything that may change their footing.

"I wanted to ask you something, priest," Petra said without turning back.

"Can't you just read my mind?" His voice was despondent, as he quickly trailed after his mental invader.

She glanced over her shoulder at him, with a gleeful grin. "I think I know," she said as she continued walking, facing Michael with her empty eyes. "But I want to hear you say it." She paused as she fell back, turning to walk by his side whilst looking at him. "Why are you not fighting? It can't just be because I took your pain away. I could be leading you to your death."

Michael laughed a sad laugh.

"Do you find your demise funny?" Petra asked, showing some rare confusion.

"I guess you were locked away for the past decade or so," Michael said. "But I've not only accepted my death, but I deserve it after what I did to you. Well, I mean the girl you took over."

"You blame yourself for me stealing her body, and you fighting with me?"

"You wouldn't understand."

"Try me."

Michael sighed as he spoke. "If I was half the priest I thought I was, I would have been able to save her. Just like I saved others before—"

"I'm going to let you in on a secret," Petra turned, stopping Michael in his tracks. The surrounding darkness was barely lessened by the cloudy moonlight that now cascaded down and cast everything in a gray hue. "You know there are no demons as you see them, don't you?" Before allowing him to answer, Petra continued. "My kind play with you. We inhabit to pass the time and pretend you have dominion over us. We play the part, then disappear. When really, we are still there. The only reason it didn't happen this time, is she was the chosen. The one who carries me to an end. The one who joins me in an eternal slumber to raise our father." She turned and began walking again. "You didn't honestly believe that your Abrahamic nonsense holds any sway in the eternal nothingness of creation, did you?"

Michael did not reply. He had lost his faith long ago. At least on the surface. He did not believe he was even worthy of believing, so had forced himself to reject all notions of it. To reject his faith, he had to also reject the life as he knew it.

"We are here!" Petra said gleefully, as she pointed at the Old Chapel coming into view through the dark clouds around them.

As they hurriedly walked up the path, dark silhouettes ahead began to drift into view through the mist. Silhouettes of many people, all stood at the bluff's edge. Each of them staring away from their approach, staring out to sea.

"I have arrived," Petra shouted at the top of her lungs as she noticed the masses that stood in font of her.

Michael shook his head as he walked up beside her. "How do you think they can hear you? You're in *my* mind."

Petra smiled yet remained looking forward, as she shouted more. "Baal has arrived. You shall all kneel before me!"

Bobbi Alderton woke up happy this morning. She did not mind the storm outside, and was more than happy to go shopping with her big brother, Andy, as well as her grandfather. Though now, things were not the same as they once had been.

Bobbi now walked down the cobbled street that ran behind the port, her eyes devoid of the personality they had once had, devoid of all of her humanity.

Beside her, Aiden Grey, the local primary school teacher—one of Bobbi's teachers, no less—walked at the same pace as her, in the same mind-set as her. Neither of them even flinched when they stepped over the fallen corpse of her brother. Her brother who still lay strewn on the road, covered by a fancy dress wizard's cape.

And from them, not one flinch, nor one care. Nothing to them was even a concern. They just had to get to their destination.

In the eyes of someone not under the spell, the town seemed heavily misted, very dark with a cold moonlight attempting to break through, threatening a new storm at any moment. Yet through the eyes of those now possessed by a malevolent mind, Port Gaynor was a different place. Very different.

In their eyes, the sea now boiled a deep bloody red.

In their eyes, the roads around them teemed with life that came from the sea. Crabs, hundreds in number, crawled throughout the town, on every road on every surface. As Bobbi and Andy walked, they occasionally stood on these creatures that happened to be in their path, cracking the poor creatures shells under their weight.

In their eyes, the Old Chapel on the hill emitted the same color red as the sea had, but now it beamed upward to the heavens, capturing the moon brightly in its glint. A beacon that called to the skies like a beckoning siren.

In their eyes, neither Henry nor Bobbi had even seen the body of Andy lying in their way. To them all there was, was the path ahead. The path to Baal, the path to Dagon, the path to sacrifice, all in the loving embrace of insanity.

As Bobbi and Andy walked up the path away, they had not noticed Emmet dragging the dazed body of Anna deeper into the woods. They only saw their prize. Their destination far ahead. Everything else was of no consequence.

Dragging their possessed focus away from their goal would only happen if they were physically interrupted. As Henry Alterton proved unwittingly to his grandson Andy, as anyone who tried to stop them faced immediate and dire consequences.

In the lower rooms of the Port Gaynor lighthouse, Emmet Jones threw his only friend—the now vicious Anna Ólafsdóttir—into the storeroom of the building. The only windowless and secure room he knew of.

As he released her neck and hurled her into the small room, she whirled, regained her balance and ran back toward him, arms clawing outward as she screamed a furious banshee wail. But she was not quick enough.

Slamming the door to the storeroom, just before she could reach him, Emmet had managed to slide the large locking bolt closed, trapping her inside of the room.

On the other side of this door, Anna furiously beat on the metal frame with her tiny arms, attacking this large object with an animalistically savage and violent madness. With no concern for her own wellbeing, Anna did not care that the skin on her hands had started to bleed from their repeated collision with a cold, heavy door.

Emmet stared at the locked door with tears in his eyes. Anna's primitive cries and growls from inside had terrified him, yet he had no choice but to help her, or at least try to.

Sitting down at the small table by a round porthole window, Emmet then closed his eyes for one moment, as he tried to process all that he had done, and what Anna had somehow become.

A banging on the inside of the storeroom door started and did not stop.

Glancing out of the porthole window, trying to force his attention away, Emmet could only see the dark clouds that had descended on the town and now crept across it, changing the townsfolk who came into contact with it.

Bang, bang, bang.

Anna's anger showed no signs of slowing or stopping.

Michael cautiously walked through the crowd of people that stood motionlessly on the edge of the bluffs, with their hands in the air, raised palm up in praise. They did not even glance at him as he walked cautiously by. They were too focused on their own fate to pay him any mind. Each of these people smiled eerily toward the dark horizon, out to the red boiling seas they saw in their eyes.

Step by careful step, Michael moved onward, careful to not touch one of these people. As he followed Petra. As he did, he felt like each one of these people were a ticking bomb. Even though he had no way to safely know for sure, he had an overwhelming feeling that if he touched one of them, interrupted what they were doing in any way, they would attack him without any hesitation.

"Why are you not kneeling?" Petra screamed loudly. "You should be praising my return!"

"How can they see you?" Michael whispered to her. "You are not really there!"

Hearing this, Petra stopped and suddenly turned on him. "You know *nothing*!" She glared at him with a disgusted expression. "I am not simply a figment of your imagination. I am not anything that you can cast aside as a fiction." As she spoke, as her anger started to form, small trails of black smoke began to seep out from her sockets, nose, mouth and ears—as well as the bullet hole wound on her forehead.

Noticing this, and knowing what that smoke had done to the orderly, and seeing the effects of it with Ólaf Hansson, Agnes Stahl and Huw Atkins, Michael relented and raised his hands up in appeasement. "I'm sorry," he whispered, trying to calm. "I didn't mean—"

Without entertaining him any more, Petra turned and walked away, the smoke ebbing from her, gradually more and more as her anger grew in its intensity.

Deputy Heather Goodridge sat in the darkness of her basement, trembling in fear.

Wearing a large gas mask over her head, and hiding in the depths of what was her bomb shelter, she clutched her police issue shotgun. She was ready for any attack.

From witnessing the events at the sheriff's station to the strange smoke that started to flood the town, Heather's online-taught survival training had kicked in speedily. She had simply run home after the doctor had woken up from death, with the sheriff seemingly in league with whatever had happened.

She had at first presumed it a contained threat. But later, when she saw that the darkness suddenly descended unnaturally upon the town—she grabbed her gas mask, without a second thought, and locked herself in the shelter under her home.

A few years ago, some neighbors who knew that Heather had converted her basement into a fallout shelter, labeled her a conspiracy theorist. A nut job. But here and now, she now more than felt justified.

She had seen on her CCTV monitors, fed from cameras positioned all around her house, that all her most hated neighbors had choked on the mist, then later stood up and walked away in a daze. She had even seen the doctor and sheriff walk by her house in that very same daze. She felt smug that she was the only one prepared for this.

"Goddamn Isis," she mumbled as she watched the people fall and rise on-screen. "I told 'em I wasn't crazy. Now who's laughing, eh?" Though, she was far from laughing. She was too terrified to laugh.

After what seemed like an age of silence, on the monitors, Heather saw something different. Military men with gas masks on, each holding guns, walked slowly and cautiously down the street behind her house, with their weapons poised.

Looking closer at the screen, she then saw the American flag emblazoned upon the arms of the camouflage pattered hazmat suits.

"God bless the goddamn United States of America," Heather grinned, as she quickly got to her feet and ran across the room to the shelter's metal door. "The cavalry have arrived."

Expecting to be met with an offer of rescue, from what she had believed to be a chemical attack, Heather did not expect the barrage of unhesitating gunfire that flew at her. Gunfire that ripped through her body in seconds, killing her where she stood. But that is exactly what happened.

And without a pause, the military presence on her street slowly moved onto the next street.

FIFTEEN

President Albert Gutierrez sat at the head of the war room table and felt like his life's work was over. Like he was making the worst mistake of not only his life, but that any president has ever made. The ultimate mistake that would signal the end of his term as well as all life.

The men around him buzzed around the room with updates from the squad in Port Gaynor. But no matter how many times Albert was told that this was all for the greater good, he could not excuse the taking of American life when it came to 'maybes'. No one knew for *sure* what was happening. No one knew for *sure* that whatever was heading to the port was a danger to anyone. No one knew *anything* except fear.

Despite this, he had given the go ahead, so whatever happened now was solely on him. It was because of this decision, that a part of him, deep inside, prayed for what was coming to justify the order. That what he had sanctioned to happen in Port Gaynor would be known in any history books remaining, that he did what had to happen.

When the dark cloud unnaturally swept in from the sea, and made its way to the other side of town, it had affected one of the soldiers standing at their makeshift post a mile from the port. Reports had soon followed that this man in question had quickly lost his mind, and began mercilessly attacking all those in his squad who had tried to stop him walking back into the cloud, and back into the town. It was then that those back in the war room realized that the town was a risk. The rest of the soldiers were quickly ordered to prepare to go beyond just containment, and instead to head into town to look for a cause. They were given the additional order to cleanse the town with extreme prejudice. To neutralize all they came across. They were told that nothing could be left up to chance.

"A clean slate's better than the alternative," the General had told the war room. "If whatever this is, is the same as what was in Europe. Then these people have been infected. You've all seen movies like this. The infected must be neutralized. What if it spread throughout the country? We don't have the luxury to know if they're not contagious with whatever they have. And if these reports we got are right, then these people are willing to die for... whatever it is they think."

"What if it's not enough?" the president asked.

"What if this won't stop whatever's coming, that's if anything's coming at all?"

"I have seen enough to know that it *is* coming," the General said as he shook his head. "And whatever it is, we have to be ready. We have to be ready to make the tough choices. This isn't about individuals. This is about the bigger picture. The soldiers are probably a useless endeavor. But they have a short amount of time to prove us wrong."

The president knew what this meant. He knew that after today, he would forever be known for his actions at Port Gaynor. He would be known as either a savior or a fool.

"You?" said the undead creature that once was Sarah Babbidge, as she turned and stared at the young Petra.

Stood at the cliff's edge, this now corrupt Sarah then chuckled. "This is priceless."

"S-Sarah?" Michael spluttered as he walked out from the crowd of the possessed, and into the small clearing where Petra now stood.

But as Sarah's attention flitted over to him, Michael could see that whatever she was, was not what stood before him now.

"Priest," she nodded. "I have a memory of you." She paused for a moment in deep thought, glanced at Petra, then back to him. "You are the one that caused all of this. Caused this abomination to be here now."

"You can see her?" he scoffed.

"Abomination?" Petra bellowed in fury. The dark wisps of smoke again poured out of her, like smoke from an old car's exhaust, with more coming out every time her anger was revved like an engine. "I.. Am... Baal!" she screamed. "You will kneel in filth for me!"

A silence settled between them as Sarah stared at the child with an amused expression.

Petra, feeling an insurmountable fury, leaked more black smoke with each grunted exhale. "Why don't you do what I command?!" she yelled.

"You honestly believe that, don't you?" Sarah replied in a calm, though gurgled tone from the trauma on her neck. As she spoke, the smile remained on her face.

"Sarah," Michael interjected, "What's happening? What happened to you?"

Sarah ignored the question and kneeled down in front of Petra, looking at her bloody eye sockets at her level.

"If you *were* Baal," Sarah said. "Then why are you stuck in a priest's mind? Baal is not one to be restrained by a human."

"If I am not Baal," Petra replied. "Then how can you see me?" Her voice sounded triumphant.

Sarah pointed out to the ocean. "Out there, coming at any moment, is the one that is Baal. And I was sent by them to come here, to meet them to offer them to their father." Her arm soon dropped. "And you? You are nothing but an echo of what was beautiful."

"I AM BAAL!" Petra screamed, the black smoke shooting out of her.

"You?" Sarah said as her tone quickly turned cruel. "You are merely a petulant memory of a girl who cannot control the remnants that a god left in their wake. The real Baal will be here soon."

"What?" Michael muttered to himself. He stood there listening, unable to do a thing. Feeling weak and impotent. He was a failed priest, a drunk, who held no sway over the powers that he now witnessed.

"I AM BAAL!" Petra screamed. "There is no other than I!"

"I gave you audience as you have the infection my god left in you," Sarah's words were quickly losing interest as she stood and turned back to the ocean. The ocean that she saw as bubbling red. "And that is all you have. You are powerless. A neutered copy of a shadow of a ghost."

Petra looked in shock. "Neutered!? I have power." She turned to Michael. "Tell her of my power!"

"She does," Michael said. He had no idea why he spoke up for this monster that dwelled in his mind. "I have witnessed it. She infected people—"

"Silence, priest!" Sarah interrupted. "Your ghost here has no more power than a baby with a gun. It may have a weapon, but cannot control it or fathom what it is." She turned to Petra with a look of disgust. "Look how your father's grace pours out of you like a river. Ebbing with the tides of your emotion. Without meaning. Without rhyme or reason. Do you know why that is?"

Petra thought for a moment, but could not find an answer in her anger.

"Because that power is not yours!" Sarah screamed. "You are what remained of the host. Trapped in the grip of my deity. And now you are free, covered in what was left after you were removed. With fractions of thoughts and a sliver of someone else's power." She then motioned with her head toward Michael. "Freed in this condition by him! He is your savior, otherwise you would be a silent voice in a prison of your real mind. You may understand the parlor tricks as your human brain can piece them together, but you cannot hold the fire with humanity."

"How do you dare to presume this?" Petra accused pointedly, her voice wavering as she struggled to maintain her confident anger.

Sarah smiled. "I have the knowledge of ancients. I may not know your name. I may not know what you think. But I have a distant memory of my own. I know what happened and my part in it. I also know Baal. I finally know my god and all they are and all they can be. And you are a mockery of what I know. You are a jester in the court of a king, playing at being royalty because you found a crown."

"No," Petra protested.

Sarah did not hear though, she was too busy smiling at the sea. "Praise Dagon, for Baal has come!" she said almost ecstatically. To which the entire crowd of brainwashed acolytes copied that phrase, repeating it over and over loudly.

"Praise Dagon, for Baal has come!"

"Praise Dagon, for Baal has come!"

"Praise Dagon, for Baal has come!"

Petra then turned to look out to the ocean, as she too witnessed what was now walking out of the waters, and onto the rocks below. "But... I am here, aren't I?" she weakly spoke, then turning to Michael helplessly. "Aren't I?" Despite not having eyes, Petra's emotional turmoil was evident.

Michael saw the truth in Sarah's word. This wasn't a god in child's form. This wasn't a devil either. This was a scared, bitten and angry child, with the remnants of a god's power and a fractured mind. That revelation hit him like a truck. He had exorcised something that day, not the monster, but the girl the monster imprisoned. And the powers she did have were not only not hers, but she had little control or understanding of.

At the bottom of the bluffs. The bloated and horrific walking horror that escaped the Vatican, the real Petra, finally stepped out of the waters and began its ascent up the cliff face. Its skin was blue and swollen, damaged from the ocean depths, as it climbed with almost zero effort up to the adoring crowds above.

"No," Petra almost cried. "I am Baal... How can I not be...?"

Sarah and the acolytes could not hear her pleas, as they busily repeated in a chorus, "Praise Dagon, for Baal has come!"

Michael quickly ran over to kneel beside the young Petra. "Listen to me, Petra—"

"Don't call me that!" she shouted, more confused than angry. "I am Baal. I *have* to be... I remember. I feel."

"I'm sorry, Petra," Michael said, holding her by her arms. "You *must* know this is true. You must *feel* it is."

Petra looked over the edge of the bluffs. "If all of this is true, then that is me. That is my real body."

Michael peered over the edge and saw the grotesquery that now scaled the bluffs up toward them. The water bloated, destroyed body of the real Petra Mayhew. The Petra that was taken, barely alive, all those years ago from this same chapel. He could see, despite the sea damage, despite the years of drink that dulled his mind, he could see in an instant that this was the human body of the real person he once tried to help. The one that was taken to the Vatican. He could even see the bullet wound on this creature's forehead as it came closer toward him on the rock face. The smoke that had come out of her from the journey now came out in small trickles.

"Dear Lord, save us," Michael said in terror, as

he backed away from the edge. Turning to the young Petra. "It is you. The real body."

From his vantage point on the lighthouse, Emmet peered through his binoculars. From on top of the main gallery, he stared down to the scene unfolding on the bluffs. He could see the man he knew as Mike the Drunk, talking to no one as he mimed dragging something away from the edge. All in front of the possessed masses. He could not see the young Petra, as she did not exist in his reality.

He could though hear the chanting, and he had a feeling that below him, in the store room, locked away, Anna was most likely chanting too.

Sixteen

S tood at the top of the bluffs, facing Sarah and her congregation, the real, water-rotten Petra glanced to her left then to her right, surveying all that had come. Her body was a vision of utter terror. With soapy, wax-like skin stretched over her bloated and water-logged body, the devastation their human casing had endured in no way affected the demon within—Just as her lack of eyes did not stop her being able to see all around her. The smoke that had billowed from her, now ebbed away. Finished in its expulsion, mainly from the weakness of the beast.

Sarah stepped forward and kneeled down in front of this monstrous grotesquery. "Praise Dagon," she said with tears of joy almost breaking through, "For Baal has come!"

"Praise Dagon," the crowd then chanted, repeating.

"NO!" the young apparition of Petra screamed,

as she and Michael stood by helplessly, having witnessed the real Petra's arrival and the start of something apocalyptic begin. "*You can't be me!*" As she spoke, the smoke started billowing out of her eyes yet again. This time thicker and quicker it escaped her.

Michael, meanwhile, slowly backed away as quietly as he could, further from off the bluffs, further from this terrifying scene.

The real Petra and Sarah did not pay either of them any mind, as the surrounding skies above, suddenly imploded into a large red storm. The mist that also covered the town also turned the same hue of crimson.

A crack of lightning illuminated the skies.

Then another.

Then another.

Strike after strike, this sheet electricity lit up the skies through the clouds, exposing what looked like something rising from the sea far, far out. A silhouette of a behemoth.

As the storm raged, the waters churned violently. The air was thick with anticipation from the gathered thrall, and the sound of the creature's movement far in the distance sounded like the grinding of the earth's plates. Michael, already grappling with his fear and disbelief, steadied himself, realizing that this was no mere myth but a horrifying reality. An actual god has arisen, albeit a dark one.

A deep booming echoed from the horizon then

swept over the land. Like a deafening demonic horn, this was the sounding of the coming of a new age, and this sound affected all humans who could hear it. Deafening them.

Before he could run, Michael fell to the floor, clutching his ears.

Before they could reach St Jude's, the soldiers that advanced through the streets, also fell down in audible agony.

The only ones unaffected were Emmet, who still watched through his binoculars on the main gallery of the Lighthouse, luckily immune to all of this monstrous control. As well as the gathered masses who also were unaffected physically, as the spell over them did not allow them to feel the pain their body may be in. They just still chanted 'Praise Dagon,' over and over again.

The heralding horn soon faded out as the real Petra then began to walk past Sarah and trod awkwardly toward the Old Chapel. Their body movements were pained as the monster in Petra was weakened after all they had been through to get here.

With a smile, Sarah removed the ornate sacrificial knife from a pocket in her ripped clothing. This, the same knife that had slit hers and Father Harris' throats. The same knife with the carved human bone handle, carved into the shape of tentacles wrapping around each other.

Out at sea, far in the distance, the bubbling red seas were now more than an illusion as Michael opened his eyes after the horn's assault, and saw the wide expanse of oceans now boiled and red, just as all those under the spell had seen for hours. The red cloud that rose above the waters, billowed outward as the lightning strikes persisted. Cracking loudly as each one flashed.

Then, the skies opened, and the red clouds unleashed a colossal torrent of rain upon the town.

In the distance, the rising leviathan, shrouded by the clouds, rose higher and impossibly higher out of the water. The darkness of this silhouette was now at least a kilometer high from the water's surface. But this thing was deep within the clouds. Not quite within the reality of humanity just yet. It stood like a monolith at the precipice of reason. Waiting for the doors between worlds to open. Waiting for the upcoming ceremony to let them through.

With the horn subsided, the only sounds were those of the rain, and the young Petra. Her anger was now mostly beyond words, as she screamed in fury as the real Petra walked away to the chapel, and as the beast in the distance loomed over them through the clouds.

Now the smoke seeping from her was getting thicker and thicker, despite the downpour upon them. Her uncontrolled power began losing any restraint she had grasped upon it before.

"Petra," Michael pleaded to her, trying to ignore the throbbing in his head from the effects of the horn's sounding. "*Please*, we have to go!" he began to stagger quickly away, beckoning her to follow him with his hand.

"NO!" she screamed.

President Gutierrez stared at the monitors in shock.

"We have no idea what it is, but it is large," a voice said. A voice the president could not place, as he was too busy feeling his whole legacy crumble.

On the screen, a satellite image showed a large mass in the water off the eastern seaboard of the United States.

"It could be aliens, couldn't it?" A voice suggested. "Like first contact?"

"It's a threat, sir," said another voice.

"You have to make a decision, Mr. President."

"Mr. President, this is no time for weakness."

"What are my options?" was all Albert could think of asking, as he then looked up to the General, who now stood beside him.

"A tactical missile strike is the only option," the General answered sadly. "And I'm talking about the *big one*. Tomahawks'll do nothing to something this size."

"Nuclear?"

The General shrugged slowly. "If we don't, we know some other country will. We already have had calls from Russia, China, France, England. All have the same information as us, and all have urged us to do something now, or they will have to, to stop whatever it is happening to them as well."

"But we *don't know* what it is," Albert said in frustration, as he turned back to the screen. "It could be good? It could be like they said, first contact? It could be just a shadow."

"First contact that left a trail of thousands dead? First contact that has decimated life in the Atlantic. That is not any kind of contact that could be good, or one we could just *allow* to happen." The General sounded gradually more impatient as he spoke. "Our men on the ground told us what was happening to the town, what happened to one of them. So whatever it is, is most assuredly against us."

"I know," Albert said in defeat, admitting what he knew aloud.

"Now we've lost all contact with our men as well," The General's voice got louder. "Whatever that shadow is, it's out to destroy us, Mr. President. No if's. No But's. We must take *decisive* action. We must use our best weapon to try to neutralize *whatever* is in there. We can't do this by half measures or with weakness."

"How can I know that this is the right thing to do?"

"Please Mr. President, this is *critical*," the General implored. "We don't have time. That thing out there, good or bad, whatever it is, is getting bigger. Just look at the satellite images? Even if whatever is in that dark spot means well, it is hurting us now. Intentions be damned. If it hurts us, we must react with force. We cannot allow that to happen. *You* cannot allow that to happen. *You* must strike. *You* must strike now."

The crowds of the faithful still stood on the bluffs. "Praise Dagon," each of them still chanted. They were focused on what was raising out to sea.

"They will *pay*," the young Petra angrily barked as she turned to the Old Chapel, where the real Petra and Sarah had now entered. "This was to be *my* sacrifice! This was to be *my* destiny!" she turned to Michael, distraught, the smoke from her eye sockets now escaping faster and fuller. "Wasn't it? Wasn't it mine?" she breathed in deeply as she tried to hold her emotions at bay. "Who am I, if not Baal? Who am I, if not the harbinger of my father? How can *that one* be what I feel I am?"

"You are Petra Mayhew," Michael said as he tried to calm her. "Baal," he said as he quickly pointed to the Chapel. "*That* Baal was the one who stole you away. The one who made you *this*. All you feel is just what was left after I... I tried to free you. But you are here. You are *you*. You just need to remember yourself. You are *not* that thing. It may walk in your body, but it is not you. It is not Petra. You are Petra."

But Petra's fury was blinding her reason. The black smoke pouring from her began to change color and consistency. Growing lighter and lighter in hue, the smoke took on a thick inky look that betrayed gravity as it floated out from her. The angrier she got, the more it came out, and paler it became.

But Petra was not listening. "They will pay in blood!" she screamed at Michael, as she then broke into a sprint, across the grass, through the old graveyard, toward the chapel after them.

But as she got nearer, and further from Michael, their bond reached it maximum distance, and he suddenly felt a jolting pull from nowhere, as her running began to drag him toward the Chapel as well. It were as if they were connected by an invisible bond that stopped the distance between them getting too wide.

Then, as all this was happening the crowd stopped their chant.

They lowered their praising hands and without any prompt, all moved en masse and at speed forward. Each of them suddenly breaking into a sudden sprint, without any hesitation, towards the edge of the bluffs.

Dozens upon dozens upon dozens of brainwashed townsfolk, suddenly fell to their deaths upon the rocks below, as each of them willfully hurled themselves off of the high cliffs.

As each body collided with the unforgivingly jagged rocks below, the red sky shimmered. As if each body that expired through their sacrifice was starting an engine.

Over and over in quick succession they jumped to their doom, and over and over as they died, the sky glowed more and more red. Like a lightning storm of blood, these suicides had started something unnatural and terrifying.

Ólaf Hansson, Huw Atkins, Aiden Grey, Bobbi Alderton, Alvin Razak. Each and every one of the damned souls followed the same fate as the rest, as their bodies fell in tribute to their god. Those that were already dead, now died for a second time. And each of them were glad to have done it.

For those that landed on other bodies upon the rocks, and did not die immediately, quickly and repeatedly butted their heads upon the rocks their broken bodies lay on, until their lives were forcibly ended by their own hand. Breaking their own heads apart to ensure their sacrifice. And each did it at such speed as if it were a race and first to die would win.

As he witnessed the mindless masses sacrifice themselves off the bluffs, Emmet had thrown down his binoculars, then run down the lighthouse's spiral staircase to the store room where Anna was being held. Needing to make sure was okay having seen those like her willingly murdering themselves.

But, when he had got outside of the room, there was no longer any banging on the door, as there had been since he trapped his friend in there. There was no longer any sound at all.

"Anna?" He had asked, placing his ear up on the cold metal door, hoping to hear any sound. "Please, answer me," his slurred, slow words were filled with emotion as he prayed to any god he knew of, even the one the crowds praised outside, that she was going to be okay. But there was nothing.

He could not stop the tears as he cried outside the room. Sliding down the wall to sit on the stone floor, he could not bring himself to look inside, he could only bawl uncontrollably. He felt that somehow she was gone, just like the ones outside, forced from their own mind and now taken from their very life itself.

"I'm sorry," he sobbed quietly, totally unaware of what was happening in the Old Chapel, or in the distance.

Then, he heard something he had not heard for years. A monstrous roar, from far out to sea. The same roar he heard many years before, the same that he heard often within the depths of his own nightmare. But now, this roar sounded clearer. More real. More present. Closer.

Within a few minutes of the president giving his reluctant order—and doing the one thing that he always promised himself that he would never be the one to do—an intercontinental ballistic cruise missile streaked through the skies, traveling at four miles a second, approaching the shadow that rose out of the waters, off the east coast of America. And it was not alone, three others flew from other directions, toward the same gigantic target.

As the population around the world remained blissfully unaware of what was happening in Port Gaynor, or what had really occurred in Italy and France, the world's leaders watched events unfold from their own respective war rooms. Each of them now silently hoped that whatever was in the middle of the sea would soon be gone, leaving the world as it was before. From democrat to dictator, each stared at the images in front of them, praying for the same thing, that this perceived threat would simply go away and leave them to their own petty squabbles they reveled in.

SEVENTEEN

"Come and be a witness," the bloated lips of the real Petra, the real Baal, said, as it stood in front of the alter within the Old Chapel, turning toward the open doors, to where the young Petra now stood enraged.

The young Petra stared at Baal with her empty eyes in total shock, with her smoke still billowing out of her, getting paler by the moment. "This cannot be," she weakly uttered.

Michael, now being dragged into the chapel twenty feet behind her, scrambled to his feet and ran in. Upon entering, he could not take his eyes away from the rancid vision stood at the head of the church; the monstrous Baal, in the older Petra's destroyed body, next to the undead, grinning Sarah Babbidge.

From his years exorcising demons in the name of god, this should have come as no surprise to him, and would be something he could be brave enough to face, just as he faced the many other monsters in the past. But that was before. That was when he was not weak. That was when he felt his god on his side. Now, now he wanted to run, yet knew he could not. With each step the young girl took ahead of him, he felt a pull at his body. Dragging him along until he got close enough to her. Somehow this figment in his mind had the physical upper hand.

"I am Baal!" the young Petra wailed. "It is *me*!"

The real Baal then raised one finger. The skin on her hand almost dripping off the bone, as they pointed at her.

"You," the monster's words bubbled in her throat as it spoke. "You were once the witness from inside this skin." Then turning, Baal then lay their body down upon the stone altar. Her eyeless stare did not once leave her younger version, who now stood in the middle of the nave in her fury. "Now," it continued. "Now you need to witness from the skin of another. Witness the glory. You are the final key to this second ceremony."

"I will destroy you all!" Petra growled, to which Sarah chuckled as she held the ornate knife in her hand. A ridiculous proposition in her undead ears.

Michael, with a sudden realization, ran up to the young Petra and spoke in hushed tones. Grabbing her, he turned her to face him. "Do they *need* you for this?"

Petra could barely concentrate on his words.

Her anger grew and grew, the smoke rushed out of her faster and faster.

"If what they said is true," he implored, "could they do this without you? What if you weren't here? What if *I* wasn't here?"

"What do you mean?" She managed to reply through gritted teeth.

"Let me die," he said. "You stopped me from that. Just release me. Then you won't be here to witness anything, if they need that."

Petra's expression grew more confused, as she wrenched her shoulders out of Michael's grasp and turned back to the altar.

"Priest," Sarah Babbidge said from behind the altar, as she stood over Baal, who now lay obediently on the stone. "Stop looking for escape. Neither of you are *needed*. Stop with your incessant need to validate your existence with an invented importance. And that child could no more remove your life than she can control those other remnants of power."

"I took his sickness away," Petra screamed.

"A parlor trick," Sarah laughed back. "Keeping a life is nothing compared to being able to take one. That is all a shadow of Baal. Now, witness the glory of Dagon's rise."

Meanwhile, in the distance, the red clouds that housed the colossal shadow of Dagon within it began to shift and spin around. The lightning inside gradually became more violent, and regular, illuminating the old god as it turned to face the town of Port Gaynor.

At the same moment, a nuclear warhead streaked across the sky and entered the red cloud toward its large target. But, instead of exploding into a devastating cloud, the rocket merely fell powerlessly, past the shadow and into the depths below, unexploded.

A few moments later, another headed for collision, and like its predecessor, fell without effect into the sea, just as it disappeared into the cloud.

The final two missiles soon suffered the same fate.

"Orate, fratres," Baal gurgled as they lay on the altar, with Sarah slowly raising her knife high above. "Ut meum ac vestrum sacrificium acceptabile fiat apud Dagon Patrem omnipotentem." the monster continued

In a second passing, the knife came down and entered Baal's thigh. There were no screams. No pain. Baal just stared up and began repeating that same phrase under their breath, over and over as the ceremony continued. "Ut meum ac vestrum sacrificium acceptabile fiat apud Dagon Patrem omnipotentem"

Sarah quickly pulled out the blade and spoke aloud as if to a congregation. "The seven shall part reality," she said as she held the blade up again. "Seven, the sacrifice of the many, has been done in your name. Now this be six for light."

The blade then came down and pierced Baal's other thigh, and was quickly removed and held high again.

"This be Five for rock."

The blade then pierced Baal's shoulder, and was resumed to its high position.

The young Petra turned to Michael. "I am not her?" She said in a confused panic. "Am I?"

Michael could barely see her face from the pale smoke that billowed out of her still.

"You're Petra," he replied once again.

"This be Four for water," came the voice from the altar.

The next knife wound was into Baal's stomach.

The young Petra slowly looked down at her hands, as she remembered the moments since she came out from the darkness of Michael's mind. "Then this, all of this hate inside. All of this death I carry. It is a disease I have been scarred with."

"This be three for rot," came the voice.

The next blade entered one of Baal's lungs

Petra slowly turned and walked further up the nave, still staring at her hands, thinking aloud as her voice grew more bitter by the syllable. "These powers are nothing but borrowed from the one who murdered my soul.

Outside, at the base of the bluffs, where the bodies of the town lay dead, even their demise could not hold their mouths back from repeating all at once, "Praise Dagon, Praise Dagon, Praise Dagon." These devoted, waiting to be consumed by the approaching deity.

"This be two for glory," came the voice from the altar. "The glory of Dagon. For when the glory is truly manifest, he shall feast on the devoted, who hath given of themselves to be one with the leviathan now rising into this realm."

"Baal killed me," Petra said through gritted teeth, as the pale smoke coming from her turned white and began pulsing with a luminescence within it. "*Baal killed me!*" She then screamed repeating, yet this time with such a force, her voice twisted into a bellowing attack. Impossibly loud. And her scream even stopped Baal muttering their ancient words.

The monster on the altar turned to her with a look of shock. Even Sarah stood staring, taken aback with her knife still raised.

Petra's smoke now grew and grew and got brighter and brighter and turned into a bright yellow fire that raised high above.

"You should not have this much power," Sarah muttered under her breath.

"*You took my world!*" Petra screamed again, as the fire from her shot outward and toward the altar. Just falling short of the monstrous ceremony. She strode forward in an uncontrollable rage. "You left me like *this!*" she continued bellowing, and with each word came more flames rising from her, shooting forward as she spoke each syllable. Getting more furious as she did.

Baal quickly turned to Sarah. "Finish it," it said loudly in its broke and gargled voice.

Getting her bearings, Sarah quickly raised the knife with forced confidence, as she tried to ignore the torment and fire and rage getting closer to them by the second.

"And this be One for Dagon," the undead woman said. But before the knife could come down, Petra shouted the last words Sarah would ever hear in both her life and death.

"*Die!*" Petra screamed, and she jumped forward. The flames from her engulfing Sarah in an instant. Within a second of this happening, the flames consumed the dry husk of her body. As her dead skin and bone were incinerated immediately, her hand lost control of the sacrificial blade and it fell down to the stone floor with a hollow clang.

Michael stood helpless to do anything except be the witness this time. But instead to the destruction of this god, not the raising of another.

Petra was now on top of Baal, not even giving the monster time enough to realize what had happened to her acolyte.

The young girl stared this monster in its face. Both of their empty eye sockets faced each other. But before Baal could use their powers, before the more powerful smoke could erupt from within them, Petra screamed her banshee wail. And as she did so, the fire from her eye sockets and mouth bellowed out into the empty eyes of Baal. Quickly filling them with her powerful fire.

Baal had no time to react.

All this happened too fast for any defense to be mounted. The journey and the wounds suffered from the ceremony had weakened them. So when fire flooded their empty sockets, the damage burned deep and burned quick. Without their full strength, Baal could only lie there helpless, as Petra's fury engulfed and consumed the remains of the body this monster had once stolen.

Out at the bottom of the bluffs, the dead were no longer chanting, but instead screamed in a torment, as the shadow in the red cloud began to fall back into the depths, and the red clouds began to lose their color and turn back into a dark and stormy shade.

Soon, their cries died out and their bodies reverted to the lifelessness that had been forced upon them.

The war room was silent.

Everyone there, from the president to the security guards, now stared at the large monitors. The screen showed trajectory lines of four missiles, all congregating on the same target off the coast of Port Gaynor.

"What the hell happened?" The president asked aloud.

The General was on the phone listening to the person on the other end with extreme intensity.

"Has it happened?" The president asked no-one. "Is it over?"

The General then replaced the receiver onto its handset and sighed in confusion. "It's gone. Whatever it was," he paused for a moment. "It's just gone."

"We destroyed it?"

The General shook his head to answer this question. "We lost contact with all four ICBMs at the point of impact. Satellite shows that none of them had delivered their payload."

The president felt a deep relief but also a creeping fear. "So, if they didn't go off," he asked reluctantly. "What happened to them?"

"We're trying to find out. But all four entered the water, then disappeared from radar."

"Sank?"

"No. We could still trace them even if they were lying on the bottom." The General then turned to the monitor and looked at the trajectory map. "Whatever we aimed at, we seemed to have missed it somehow, and then... they all vanished. As did the target."

The president did not reply. He just looked down at the desk and could not help but worry about where the missiles went, and whether whatever the thing was, had really gone.

He felt a strong sinking feeling that someday, he

would learn the answer to these questions, and he would regret ever giving the order.

Little did he know that his feeling was indeed correct, as deep in a thick mist of fire and ice, four nuclear explosions occurred across a begotten landscape close to our reality. The dry land cracked, as did a veil separating the two worlds, and through the cracked dirt, under the looming mushroom clouds, sea water began to rise up. Sea water not from their world but from ours.

"Emmet?" a weak voice called out from the lighthouse store room. Anna.

"Where are you?" She called out again.

Emmet's eyes lit up as he smiled.

Michael found himself lying, face down on the concrete floor of the Old Chapel. The building around him now lay in a destroyed ruin from the attack that Petra had wrought.

His ears rang, and he felt a wooziness.

His lungs felt tight with the dust and smoke he inhaled.

His eyes stung as he rubbed the debris away

from them, unable to stop the aggravated tears streaming from them.

Moving a shard of wood from a splintered pew off of his legs, he then clambered to his feet, getting his bearings.

He did not know all of what had happened, as the last thing he saw was a light of fire roaring out of Petra's body, onto the weakened Baal. That fire had shot out and ripped through the pew and walls around him.

Looking up, he noticed the roof of the chapel was now mostly missing, and outside the torrent of rain had gone. A clear night sky above allowed moon and starlight to trickle into this smokey ruin.

He could not feel the pain that he had in the hospital, so he knew that Petra was still here, within his mind. He could not begin to fathom how something unreal could do something like this, but he had seen the powers at play and knew his own experience was infantile compared to what could indeed happen with gods and monsters.

"Petra?" Michael called out as he made his way over the ruined pews, toward the altar, that shrouded in the thickest smoke and debris.

"Petra?" He repeated.

He did not know why he was looking for her. She may not be Baal, but she was still monstrous. Yet if she was indeed the girl that he had tried to save, and was twisted by the evil that took hold of her, then he *had* to help her.

He had failed his god, but he would not fail this child, even in her cursed death.

As he stepped around the fallen remains of the chapel roof that lay in shards, Petra came into view.

Still stood on the altar, she looked the same as she had when she first appeared in his mind. Still a grotesque sight with bloodied eye sockets and wounds all over her body, but nothing here had affected her.

She stared down at the altar, upon which, at her feet, a dark shadow was burned into its stone. This was the remains of Baal. This was where Petra's real body had been destroyed.

"Why do I remember so much, if I am not Baal?" She asked weakly. "Why am I cursed like this?"

"I don't know," Michael replied, stepping closer to the altar.

She turned to him, and for the first time, Michael saw beyond the horrific visage. He saw the innocence beneath. The innocence that remained.

"But we do know one thing," he continued.

She stared at him helplessly, needing some comforting words.

"You beat it," he said. "You won over it, didn't you? So you are not powerless like they said."

Petra thought for a few moments before speaking. "I want revenge," she said.

"Didn't you get that?"

"No. I want it on all of them." Her words were quiet, yet strong.

"What are you saying?"

"We can find them all, no matter where they hide, can't we?" she then turned and stepped off from the altar, and stood in front of Michael, looking up at him "We're stuck together?" She reached out and held his hand. "And I don't want to die, do you?"

Michael smiled back, he was not sure why he smiled. But he did.

EPILOGUE

Port Gaynor, in the wake of an apocalyptic storm, found itself wrapped in an eerie calm. The dawn broke with a deceptive normalcy, as if the town had woken from a collective nightmare. But there was no one to wake with it. The bodies of the townsfolk remained spread across the rocks at the bottom of the bluffs. The dark clouds that had poisoned their minds were now all gone, with the clouds that brought the storms also a memory. The summer sun had finally crept above the horizon. Despite being a stranger to the town for a long time, it now hung proudly in the sky, basking the deserted town in its warm embrace.

Aside from Michael, Petra, Emmet and Anna, the only people who were within the town to witness this new bright dawn were the soldiers sent to contain these horrors. Those sent on a mission to commit atrocities in order to save many. But as each one of these men woke up from the unconsciousness where they had fallen, each quickly sensed a change in the air. A change that had gone from a town of terror and confusion, to one of normality and renewal. Another natural day, in a boring town where nothing should ever have happened.

Life across the world soon resumed its mundane rhythm, with the horrors that Baal brought, relegated to the realm of whispered legends and fading memories. The scars, both physical and psychological, were hidden beneath the veneer of daily routine and forced forgetfulness. Even those who would now live in the towns and cities that Baal had decimated would not question what had happened. From news reports of gas leaks, to terrorist attacks, all mysteries would be given a new villain to blame. A villain tailored for that event, one that humanity could fathom, concocted by the powers that be, to distract the people from knowing the dark, terrifying truth.

Yet beneath the apparent tranquility and lies, the remnants of the supernatural still lingered. A silent testament to the thin veil separating reality from the unknown that threatened to herald a new age without human life.

For those who had witnessed the events and survived, those that had witnessed the world's approach to damnation, nothing would ever be the same; for they knew that before long, ancient powers would stir again and rise to blot out the sun with its prophesied grasp.

As the sun rose higher, casting its light on the unassuming town, the people of Port Gaynor carried on, unaware or unwilling to acknowledge the darkness that once threatened to consume them, and might yet lie in wait.

OTHER TALES

THE THING IN THE BAY

Though previously published in HorrorScope: A Zodiac Anthology: Volume 3, *I am publishing it again here, as thematically it has a lot in common; old gods, acolytes, madness.*

"Notice to all Aquarians," Alice smirked as she read aloud from an old newspaper. "The stars have aligned to shower you with charm and enchantment. Your confidence and charisma will be irresistible to those around you, but beware, for things are not what they seem. Get ready for a spine-tingling adventure."

Lowering the paper onto her lap, she sighed loudly as she muttered to herself. "Spine-ripping nightmare, more like."

It wasn't Alice's fifty years on this planet that had left her feeling so exhausted that she could almost collapse; she was in the prime of her life, at least she had been the week before. As a fitness fanatic, she lived healthily, worked healthily, and cared for each and every part of her body. She took up any and all wellbeing fads she came across, in the hope they would make her that much fitter. Even mentally, she took care of herself, and saw a therapist and a life coach at least once a month.

Alice had no family ties, nor did she want any. She had her dog, Leo, an overtly angry pug, and that was enough.

With all of that in consideration, if you had asked her a week ago, she would have told you that her life was perfect.

But this was not a week ago.

The relentless nightmarish experience of the last few days now led to her sitting on the dirty floor of this decrepit, candlelit mausoleum.

As she let out a sigh, she realized she could smell herself, and it was an unpleasant smell. But one she could not avoid. She had had no choice but to wear the same clothes ever since that governmental newsflash screamed out of her phone, and not like she had remembered to pack a wash bag as she ran for her life.

That morning when she fled her apartment, was also the same morning she had lost her job. If the world hadn't fallen down around her, she may have been sad about that, but not like she had time to care about any of that.

She did though feel ashamed of the unsanitary condition she was now in, despite none of it being her fault. No one in the same predicament as her could expect to smell like roses after what had happened. But despite her feelings of shame, she also knew that cleanliness was a thing of the past, at least for now, and it would get worse before she could find a bar of soap or some deodorant.

Now, she just tried all she could to stay awake. It had been forty hours since she had last slept, and each second she fought that slumbering darkness was a concerted battle she felt ill-equipped to win.

"You read my horoscope, so can I read yours?" David asked, extending his hand toward Alice. Sat on the floor opposite her, David did not look nor smell any better than she did. His clothes were battered and dirty. His eyes were heavy and bagged. A small man, David was stick-thin, bald, and carried with him a prematurely old demeanor.

Without a word, Alice passed the battered old paper over to him with a weak smile. As he took it, she felt glad she had run into this man. Even though she didn't know him, she doubted she could do any of this alone. And this man was seemingly the only male human left in the area— the only sane one anyway, the only one not trying to murder her.

Staring at the old newspaper, David squinted as he tried to make out the date through the grime that clung to the front page. "This is old," he said. "Fifteen year's I think."

"Does it matter?" Alice shrugged. "Not like they're gonna publish any new ones." Her expression faltered momentarily as a wave of sadness washed over her. "All of them should now just say in big bold letters, 'You're all fucked'."

Noticing her sadness, David quickly smiled to keep the mood between them light. "What star sign are you?"

"I don't really know," Alice lied, knowing full well what astrological sign she was born under. But for some reason, she felt the need to hide that fact, as if knowing it would make David think less of her. Or maybe she just hated her life in that arena. What difference would it make if she told him her star sign? So what if he even found out that she had earned a living writing those predictions for all the lowest tabloids? So what if he even discovered that the famous Shaman Bob was, in fact, her, and the man in the picture was simply, a paid actor? Not like any of it mattered. Not anymore. She had hidden her career from everyone she met, fearing that they would misjudge her for believing in such a silly subject, on that she viewed as a fiction writing job.

"You must know what sign you are," David persisted. "Everyone does!"

She had found it funny when she had read that old horoscope aloud to this man. It was one that she knew she had to have written herself, but had no recollection. She chalked that up to it being fifteen years ago, during her drinking phase. The phase that nearly ruined her.

"Fine, whatever, I'm Cancer," she suddenly relented.

As she watched David smile, then look down at the newspaper, she started to feel the warming pull of sleep, slowly taking a grip on her.

David scanned the horoscope section laid out in front of him. He couldn't help but be amused by the picture of the person who wrote them—a chubby face that grinned out from the top of the page. The man wore a sparkling fez atop his large head. The headline beside the photo read, Shaman Bob predicts your week.

"Come on, Shaman Bob," David whispered as his eyes scrolled down to the Cancer entry. "Ah, here we go," he spoke with genuine joy. He glanced up at Alice, and noticed her eyes were starting to close as she struggled to stay awake.

"Alice!" David said louder, his tone firm and sharp, jolting her awake. "You gotta stay awake with me!"

In a panic, Alice then scrambled to her feet with her eyes forcefully wide. She quickly began pacing around the small tomb, fighting the exhaustion. She looked over at the half-burned church candle they had placed in the center of the room. "This light ain't helping!" she motioned to it. "It makes this place feel like bedtime!"

"We just can't sleep," David spoke apologetically. "We really can't. You know that."

Alice shook her head dismissively. "I know, I know. But it's gonna happen at some point, right? Maybe we can open the door, get some light in. Some fresh air would keep up alert." She motioned around at the windowless stone walls. "This place is... Well, a tomb. And they have got to have left by now, right? We haven't heard from any of them in hours."

"Maybe... But maybe we should wait a few hours more," David's happier tone returned as he continued, "But not before Shaman Bob gives you your Horoscope."

"His fifteen-year-old Horoscope, you mean?"

"Yup!" David's eyes returned to the newspaper as he read aloud. "Cancer. I am sorry to tell you this... But brace yourself for an otherworldly and harrowing revelation." David's smile fell as he spoke; his voice slowed down and lost its strength with each word he uttered. "The stars foretell a cataclysm on the horizon—the end of all things loom." He paused briefly as he glanced at Alice.

"Very funny," she smirked, too tired to properly laugh at what she saw as a joke in very bad taste.

However, David was not amused at all; he looked disturbed as he helplessly scanned the rest of the words in the newspaper before him.

He quickly continued reading aloud, "As the darkness descends, an ancient, slumbering one will rise from the abyssal depths. And your life as you know it shall end." He gulped in fear as he felt a cold shiver run down his throat and his gut lurched.

"Oh, haha!" Alice sighed with a smile, but it

soon dropped as she saw his expression remain disturbed and his gaze stuck to the newspaper.

"I'm really not kidding, Alice," he spoke softly. His eyes were now transfixed on the last unread line as he whispered, "This... this can't be."

As she watched this man, this stranger, read that paper with such worry, Alice wondered to herself if he was still safe to be around. She had only met him a day or so ago. He could be anyone, after all. Their paths had crossed at the entrance to this cemetery. She didn't even know his last name. He had said he was thirty but he looked, spoke, and acted like someone much, much older. She had never even questioned any of that, not until right now.

Before her worry about him grew any more, he handed the newspaper to her, open to the horoscope page. It was then she noticed tears dripping down his cheek. "Please," he said. "Read the last line... I... Can't."

With trepidation, Alice reached out and took the newspaper from him. She glanced down at the page, and re-read the section for Cancer.

As she silently stared at the words on the page, shock consumed Alice as she saw the same unbelievable fortune David had said aloud. Her lips mouthed each syllable quietly, but stopped as her eyes hit that last line. She could not mouth those words. She was not able to.

In an instant, she dropped the paper and glared at David, who still wept silently.

"You stay there!" she commanded in fear as she backed away toward the mausoleum door.

Before she could try to gather any more thoughts through the swirling panic that filled her mind, the large, wooden door split open, and a giant red claw burst in from the outside.

Cancer - Your week ahead

That word stared at Alice from her laptop screen.

The cursor blinked away, almost mocking her writer's block.

It had been a week of a stalemate between her and her writing. Now she was two days past deadline, and she could do nothing to solve the blank page.

On the actual day of the deadline, her phone wouldn't stop ringing. So much so, that she had switched it to silent and just stared at the tiny machine illuminate endlessly when her editor kept calling. Those calls soon stopped as the 5pm deadline hit. She knew that the final warning she had received only a few weeks ago would now be converted to a dismissal. Not that she blamed them for doing any of it. She had missed countless deadlines for the best part of a year, and this week's assignment was her last chance, and not only with her publisher, but with her agent and editor too. This was the final chance she was given to pull herself out of the quagmire, but she blew it. If

Shaman Bob wasn't her creation, or wasn't so popular, she would have been fired many years ago. It was obvious now that the fame was overspent, and they did not need her or Bob anymore.

She just had nothing left to give, yet could not bring herself to tell anyone. She hated the lies her horoscopes told and always had done. The fact she was paid well to tell people these lies, ones she knew people believed, now sickened her, when once she found it all funny.

She wasn't ready to tell anyone she had had enough, though. Not yet. Not today. Even past the deadline, she tried to force the invented predictions out of her, but to no avail. Even though she knew she had been fired, she wanted to at least try to finish her work.

For twenty-three years, she had been writing these weekly horoscopes. Predictions that were republished across seventeen newspapers, as Bob was a celebrated icon. But for the past year, her predictions had either not been completed or were just so incoherent that her editor needed to re-write them himself.

"If you don't make the deadline, we'll find someone to replace Bob." That was the last words she had heard from her editor.

Shaman Bob. That damn name. The name she came up with as a joke when she started.

She stared at the cursor flicking on and off at her, mocking her with each flash.

Slowly her hands moved over to the keyboard and typed.

Cancer... You are fucked. Your life is over. This is the end of everything.

That's my last prediction, she mused.

Before she could sink into any more self-deprecation, her phone rang. Despite its silent setting, a foghorn blare emanated loudly from its small speaker, causing her to jump. A large red sign illuminated its screen.

Emergency Alert: Imminent threat to life. Object off the San Francisco Bay, USA, causing catastrophic damage through audible pulses. Nothing more is known. Damage spreading worldwide. Survival chances are unknown. May god have mercy on us all.

She read that alert slowly. Over and over. Shocked.

Her eyes could not believe those words.

Before she could even turn to look out the window or flick on her television, a second emergency alert sounded. Piercing the brief silence and making her jolt a second time.

Emergency Alert: PRAISE HIM. PRAISE HIM. PRAISE HIM.

Quickly, she turned on the TV. Each channel was dead air. Every single one showed either static, a black screen, or a 'back soon, technical issues' style notice.

Grabbing her phone, she tried to return her editor's earlier call, intending to ask him about this alert. She realized how sad it was that she only had him to ask, but with no one else, what choice did she have? Her mother had quite advanced dementia, so asking would be useless, even though she had not spoken or seen her in many years. She had no real friends to speak of. Her editor was the only person in her life that she could think of to call in an emergency, even if she knew that he was just going to shout at her about that damned deadline.

"James!" she exclaimed in relief, as the call was picked up.

Silence.

"James? Hello? Are you there?" Her voice trembled as fear crept in.

There was nothing for a few moments, not until she heard a quiet high-pitched giggle. One she could tell belonged to him.

"James, d'you get an alert?" she asked in a panic.

The laugh then continued until it turned into maniacal words.

"Praise him," he replied as his laugh surrounded each word until it turned into deafening hysterical laughter. "Praise him, praise him, praise him," he roared.

The following twelve hours were a blur.

Alice could not remember what made her drop the phone and flee her apartment. She did not remember what the catalyst was that made her pick up her dog, Leo, and run as fast as she could from the safety of her home.

She also did not remember what came first... the plane falling from the sky and exploding on the horizon, the images on all the socials of that thing rising out of the Bay, or her neighbors trying to attack her while screaming the words 'Praise Him'. Whichever order it happened, each one was enough a reason to make her leave in a panic and try her best to run anywhere safe. Her first thought, the hospital. There had to be help there, right?

As she ran in a terrified daze through the streets, her mind replayed the last thing she typed. Cancer... You are fucked. Your life is over. This is the end of everything.

And it indeed was.

Leo had managed to jump out of her hands and run away as Alice had tried to crawl over a fence leading to the back of the hospital. Without looking back, his tiny, stumpy paws made him run back in the direction they had come. In the direction of the apartment.

"LEOOOOO" she screamed. But her dog did not hear. He was gone, having disappeared without any intention of heeding his owner's pleas. Alice would have run after him if not for the horde of patients, nurses, and doctors that suddenly began pouring out of each one of the hospital's doors and windows. At every opening they appeared, screaming, laughing, yelling 'Praise Him.' They all flooded out of any exit without a single care for what floor they happened to be on, or for any damage they caused themselves from a fall. It was pure, unadulterated chaos. They were chaos.

Alice watched helplessly from the other side of the fence as she witnessed the people that survived leaving the building, then turn on each other, and literally begin ripping at one another, all whilst appearing like they were enjoying every single second of the experience. Some even began having sex with each other, while clawing at each other's eyes. Some were alone, and ripping out their own intestines then eating them. It quickly became an insane party of sex, violence and terror.

"This way!" came a voice from behind her.

Alice turned and saw a small bald man, smiling through his fear, crouched as he hid behind a bush, away from the line of sight of any of the rutting insane on the other side of the fence.

"Quick!" he commanded, but as he did, his eyes widened at the murderous crowd outside the hospital stopped in their tracks. Stopped running and turned to each other.

Alice glanced back to see what was happening.

The people... What was left of them, anyway, began... changing. More specifically, things were coming out of them, bursting out of their bodies, leaving the skin shells ripped on the grass beneath them.

As these insane, mutilated people laughed, mauled and mated, parts of their bodies split wide open, and from the wounds, huge things emerged in a fury.

Massive iterations of typically much smaller animals... Scorpions, crabs. Spiders—All with pincers and stingers that were all impossibly gigantic—clawed their way out of these people's bodies.

Before Alice could take in any more, the small man then grabbed her by the arm and pulled her away.

As she sprinted, Alice could have sworn that she heard a lion's roar in the distance behind them, among the sound of laughing screams, as well as the clacks and clicks of large pincers.

The colossal claw burst through the mausoleum door and grabbed around Alice's midsection. She screamed as the monstrous pincer cut into her skin.

Following that, a loud scuttling of legs became deafening as this monstrous crab tried its best to break through the door from the outside. Frantically scrambling against the wood to push it inside.

As Alice screamed in pain, part of her mind found the situation strangely hilarious. Despite the violence now being met upon her, her yells quickly turned to a hearty laugh. She couldn't help it.

Then she remembered the last line of that old horoscope. The one that had filled both her and David with fear. The words neither of them could speak of. Those old, printed letters on the dirty newspaper that read—'Alice... I know you are reading this... You must praise Him. Praise Him. Praise Him'.

She realized almost instantly, as she turned and saw the monster cutting into her, that what was happening was madness. Pure and feral madness.

Unable to get the rest of its body inside, the terrifying crab then released its grip on Alice. She fell to the stone floor, with her stomach bleeding from the considerable laceration the claw had made.

Outside, the raucous screams of so many wild things echoed. Things that were beyond angry. Things that were furiously and murderously primal.

In her pained daze, Alice looked up toward David, expecting to see him cowering in fear in a corner of the mausoleum. But she did not.

She did not see him at all.

He was not there.

The mausoleum was empty.

There was no David.

No candle.

No dirty, old newspaper.

As she stared into the empty stone room, she could not help laughing again.

Getting to her feet, she glanced down at her belly, at the wide gash across it, as it bled down onto her pants.

She could hear the crabs outside, but she could

not see the bloody knife gripped in her fist. The knife that she had wounded herself with.

"This is the end of everything," Alice said quietly with a chuckle, as she turned. Knowing she had to go meet the fate that awaited her.

In her eyes—her eyes that had fast become a milky, pale color—she saw monstrous entities filling the graveyard— crabs, scorpions, bulls, lions, goat-creatures, and many more bizarre visions of impossibility.

Her laughter soon grew louder as the scene played out. She stood there, bleeding heavily, watching the symbols of each sign of the zodiac, in a large and terrifying form, attacking everything in sight.

Those things. They were all astrological, and she found that hilarious.

And through her laughter, she began her chant, as if on instinct. "Praise Him. Praise Him. Praise Him. Praise Him."

Meanwhile, Leo, Alice's beloved dog, watched his owner through the gate of the graveyard. His animal eyes took it all in; his owner laughing to herself, stumbling outside the mausoleum, stabbing herself in the stomach. His brain could not fathom what was happening. All of the people he saw that day were doing the same strange things that he could not comprehend.

Those few days of humanity were confusing to all of the witnessing animal population—tame and wild alike—they could only stand back and witness these cataclysmic events as they unfolded around them. They did not know of the thing in the San Francisco Bay. They had not been affected by the sound that that thing had created. A sound which had crept around the globe, scrambling the brains of humans in its path, inverting any sanity they had. The animals could only witness all of this silently.

As the last human fell down dead, and that thing in the bay receded into the murky depths, the animals would soon carry on with their lives.

They would soon forget about humans, who were now merely easy pickings for food, and instead would adapt to what the world soon become. What it once was—a land without the pestilence of humanity.

Leo, though, did not immediately accept this coming new world on his animal instinct. He had come back to find Alice. He wanted to see his friend. He loved her, as much as his small brain could allow. And as he stood watching her demise. As her laughter faded, and she collapsed to the dirty graveyard ground, Leo waddled happily through the metal gate, over to her.

In the last moments of Alice's life, through the insanity that clouded her mind, she soon recognized her dog ambling over to her. Her madness faded for a second and couldn't help but smile. Not in a scary or odd way, but a smile that was honest and loving. Seeing him dragged her memory back to sanity for a few last moments.

As Leo licked her face and as her heart beat its last, a tear fell down Alice's face.

"Leo... My little lion," she managed to utter through her breath. "Don't be scared my little one... I have your prediction for you... My real last prediction, and the only one I know to be true. Your life shall be beautiful and full of adventure..."

And as if by happenstance, that prediction was the only one she ever foretold that was 100% accurate.

THE GHOSTS OF POWICK BRIDGE

This was something I wrote as an exercise back in the depths of the first COVID lockdown. I wanted to write a short story, but with the feel of a poem; where not everything is explicit, and some things are for the reader to feel, as oppose to totally understand. I call it 'prosetry'. (I don't really, I just made that last bit up.)

As the moon rose and the light escaped for yet another night, hope it seemed, had left the bridge.

To any unsuspecting visitor who would choose to walk over the bridge's cobblestones, it may just seem slightly colder than normal. They would assume that the sudden drop in temperature and the feeling of dread were somehow due to the river Teme that ran underneath. That maybe it was a cause for the unease they would fleetingly experience.

But for these visitors, if, in the middle of such a night, they would choose to stop for a few moments on that bridge, they would find themselves feeling a lot more than slight emotional discomfort, they may see the dead.

When I first saw the bridge at the end of the dirt road, I held a gun in my hand. I was ordered, alongside my friends, to lie in the undergrowth either side of that long stretch of dirt and stone. Ordered to wait for the enemy that headed toward the bridge, and when they were all in sight, we were to unleash a fury. To steal their lives at a point blank range, all in the name of a cause that few really understood.

What followed was something that devastated me to think about, but think about it, I must. Not like there is any choice in that matter. I see it every moment of my existence. Over and over, I relive what we did, what we *all* did. What we did on the stone of Powick Bridge.

I don't know exactly when it was anymore. I don't even know how I died. I just know that this is my damnation.

One thing I know is that there is no god in heaven looking over us, for what god would condemn a man for following orders and knowing no better? No, there is no god, and if there ever was, then he is the very Devil that sits on hell's throne.

"Fall in line, for the Lord Protector," were the last words I heard before the noise of war smothered all humanity from us.

Then darkness fell as the canons roared. And somehow, *somehow*, in the moments that led up to the last breath escaping my lungs, I swear I heard a song. I'm not sure how that was possible as it was only September, but I heard I did, as clear as day. And not just any song, but one sung by a tiny voice. A hauntingly beautiful refrain. I remember hearing that as I lay in wait in the undergrowth, and as our targets passed on the road, I paused.

As my brothers in arms fired their shots, damning their targets to an immediate death, I had paused. I heard the singing. Then I swear I then saw snow falling around me. I never actually fired one shot. And when the battle moved to the bridge, I was just there, defending myself. Unsure of what to do. It was not like I was a soldier. I was just a conscript in a very uncivil war.

Time passes differently for the dead, for it is not a linear procession of hours, but a blur of confusion. Day doesn't follow night, for it is always night. All that changes is the land on which we walk on. We exist in a constant spin from reliving our demise. At least, that is how I perceived it. Time is a constant spinning wheel. It is cyclical. What was, is still, what is, always was. You only appreciate that when you exist, as I do. You don't question it, you just know that you are here, but there is no feeling of progression.. it all just *is*. For it all happens at once, not in a line. At least that is all that made sense until she arrived.

It was winter again. I could not tell you when, but the snow was thick, and the river was almost frozen.

I saw that small girl stepping onto the cold bridge, and for whatever reason, she decided not only to stop, but to sit down amongst the snow.

She did not feel the sudden cold of being in the presence of the dead, as she was too cold as is, and did not feel the dread others did. I could not warn her away from this place, as I was in the midst of my own eternity, with the other damned.

I did not know how long she had been there. Minutes, hours, or if she had always been there.

But then she saw me.

She looked up, wide eyed, and stared with a kindly smile across her small face.

"Don't be scared," she said in a tiny voice.

Those words bit through the deafening barrage of my personal war, and made me do something I had never done before my time here. I stopped the fighting.

As I did so, and turned to the girl, my enemy still fought as if I was there, with no idea that they were stuck battling the empty air, for they were on their own path, reliving this most uncivil of wars.

I turned as if it was something I always could,

yet never tried to do before, and those wide, innocent eyes were looking back at me.

Then, after what seemed like an age, she stood up to face me.

And as she had stood up, I saw she was like me, with her body being barely a whisper, as the snow fell through it.

"Don't be scared," the girl said again, as her translucent body stepped through the battle on the bridge and came to a halt in front of me.

"Let us sing," she said as she took my hand.

I did not reply. I did not know if I even could.

Slowly I walked off the bridge, led by this child, leaving the ghostly battle far behind.

Down the road we walked, she began singing that haunting refrain. The same one I had heard as the bullets fired up on me on my last day.

Around us, the snow continued to fall, as we walked off the track and into an enormous field leading towards the town. A field that I had never trod before, but one where I was, and would always be.

Stopping close to the river's edge, the girl stopped her singing and pointed to the ground I stood on.

"Don't be scared," she said again.

In a field, in the depths of a winter long ago, a small girl and her mother stood on the same ground as the snow fell around them. They looked down at a small wooden post embedded in the soil in front of them.

"Don't be scared," the mother said to her child as she looked sadly over this unmarked grave. "Your father was a brave man. He would want you to be brave too."

"Can I sing him a song?" The child weakly asked.

The mother smiled. "Of course."

The song, that haunting refrain, was sung through tears and grief, as the snow continued to fall.

Time is a circle. What was, always was, and what is, will always be. I was always alive, I was always dead. The song she had sung would always be sung. And her words would always be.

As I turned toward Powick Bridge, I saw the battle still raging as it always did, and I saw myself still there. Still fighting, always fighting. Still in my own hell, always in my own personal hell.

The girl looked up at me, and for a moment I remembered her, and saw myself in her eyes. Behind her, I then saw another figure smiling at me. And for the briefest of seconds, I remembered her beautiful face too, as the love I left.

But as fast as I recalled, the memory was lost again, and I was standing back on the bridge.

As they both faded, I lay on the ground, where my body dwelled far below.

As I closed my eyes, I felt the snow falling onto my face stop, and I tasted copper in my mouth. My body seared with pain. My head span. I opened my eyes again, and the night disappeared as the setting sunshine flooded my sight with orange and red hues.

"He can't be helped," I heard a man say that stood above me. "Not with a wound like that."

My eyes shifted to the left, toward the bridge, and I saw bodies of the dead being lifted onto carts by some of my wounded brothers.

"Don't be scared," I heard the child say.

"Don't be scared," I heard the mother say.

I then heard that song again, calling me away, sung by both of them.

Time is not the same for the dead, for when close to death, time can be an eternity wrapped in a minute.

Then, as the song stopped, and the daylight faded, so did I, and the ghosts of Powick Bridge were what they always were, a memory that exists, but no longer for me.

If any visitor walks on the bridge and stops for moment, you may hear the song, you may feel an unease as death lays in those surrounding fields, you may even feel snow on your face on a summer's day. But you will feel that without me, for I will always be there, and yet never be there again, as time for the dead does not exist.

E AND THE NIGHT BEFORE CHRISTMAS

For fans of The Dead Woods, *yes this is starring THAT Sheriff Eddis Eaves-Eagleton. And yes this IS set in the same town of Hemlock Creek. But this is not a YA tale... Far from it.*

DECEMBER 24TH, 1975

For the last seven days, Storm Herra had battered the small township of Hemlock Creek. The blizzards and gales it subjected the small hamlet to, were intense and relentless, so much so that it was commonplace for residents to jovially mention the word 'apocalyptic' when describing it. All businesses had more or less shut their doors, as all anyone could do was wait the storm out and not to mention celebrate the festive season. For children, it was a gift. An extended holiday break, but for adults it was stressful.

Sheriff Eddis Eaves-Eagleton—E to his friends, E even to his enemies—sat in his patrol car outside 932 Amberson; the Eckwiss residence.

Answering a 10-71, shots fired call, would normally be a cause for alarm, but he was sure this was a mistake. *Storm Fever* he called it. When the public would go crazy from being locked up. Like cabin fever, but much more annoying, as he and his men had to answer every call, and on a night like this, he resented every call that came in.

E never had cause to come to this house before, yet he knew the owner well enough to say 'howdy' when passing on the street.

He sighed as he peered out the windshield at the raging blizzard that consumed his view. Why did he even volunteer to be the one to come out here? He was the sheriff, after all, he had deputies for all the scut work. Sure, he hated the incessant Christmas cheer in the police station, but couldn't he have endured the off-key carols being sung for a bit longer? Not then he couldn't, but now, he thought, he should have just grinned and bore it a while longer.

But it wasn't just the carols. It was what else Christmas brought him: the *Santa* comments. With his long gray and white beard and plump physique, everyone relished making the parallel between him and St. Nick. Sure, he was fat. Sure, he had a beard. But he had something Santa didn't have; the ability to fire them or shoot them. However, this mockery was not just from his deputies and the station staff; it was from anyone he met.

He should cut off his beard, he often mused. *That would stop them.* But he never did. He wondered if part of him secretly loved the attention.

Either way, here and now, he had taken the call, and now sat outside this house.

He knew how this would go. He would barge his way through the storm until he got to the Eckwiss house. He'd no doubt be met by someone who would then explain that there was no gunfire at all. That the sound must have been a car backfiring or fireworks, or a film being played too loud. Then they would make that goddamn Santa comment. He would then do what he always did, smile as politely as he could. Though it never hid his real annoyance. His aggravation was evident, despite the thin attempt at smiling. Then he would bid his goodbyes, all whilst daydreaming that he could have drawn his gun and smashed their noses in with its handle.

Peering through the thick snowfall, he could not see many signs of life in the neighboring houses. No lights. No signs of activity at all.

Grabbing the radio handset from the dashboard, E spoke gruffly as he clicked the talk button. "Agnes?" He moaned. "Who called in the 10-71? There's bupkis out here."

He only had to wait a few seconds as the station secretary soon responded, a voice E always loved to hear. The voice of his beloved wife, Agnes. In her sixties, she was also the station's switchboard, who had managed all police calls for the last 3 decades.

"Just get in there, you lazy ass!" Her annoyed voice echoed out from his radio speaker.

"Answer my question first, ya ol' witch!" he retorted with a grin.

"Fine!" Agnes said, her tone now more pleasant. "Guy never identified himself. Just called it in. Said there was someone with a gun in the house. Gave the address, then hung up."

E shifted in his seat, getting ready to open the car door and brave the elements. "Well, I'm goin' in. Love ya."

"Fuck you, sheriff," Agnes replied.

Putting the handset down, E smiled. He sure loved his wife. He loved everything about her. He especially loved how everyone thought her constantly telling him to go fuck himself was anything except a sign of love.

Putting on his wide-brim sheriff's hat that rested on the passenger seat, E then readied himself. He sucked in his enormous belly that had pressed up against the steering wheel and opened the driver's side door.

Though his girth had shrunk recently thanks to that new diet his wife forced on him, his uniform was still tight, and he was yet not an easy fit for this car. Soon, though, he had to believe. The weight loss would happen soon.

Pushing the car door open wide with force,

battling against the winds trying to shut it, E thrust himself out into the heart of Storm Herra.

As the wind noisily blasted around him, it forced the door to slam shut behind him.

With the howling wails so deafening, E wondered how in the world anyone could hear gunshots. Before he could ponder this thought any more, the wind gusted again with aplomb, ripping the hat from off his head and dragging it up through the air, swallowing it into the snow-filled veil of night.

"Mother bastard!" E shouted enraged, chastising himself somewhat. But no one could witness his swearing, as his voice was lost in the storm.

Rookie mistake, he moaned silently to himself. Agnes would have a field day mocking him about this. Must have been the tenth hat he lost this year.

For a fleeting moment, he considered chasing the hat down, but with the chill getting colder and the snow getting more blizzardy, he didn't want to stay out too long. He had a job to do.

Turning to 932 Amberson, E squinted and gritted his teeth. His beard fluttered over his shoulder against the oncoming wind. With each step he took toward the porch, a new battle was fought between him and Storm Herra. But he was determined *that bitch* (as he referred to it) would not win against his 320lb body, as it did with his hat.

As he approached the porch, the shroud of

snowfall thinned, blocked by the frame of the house. E could now see clearly that the front door was wide open. Judging from the amount of snow in the hallway inside, he could tell it had been open for a while.

Instinctively, E's hand grabbed the pistol from off of his belt. He could see these warning signs, and he hadn't lasted over 40 years in law enforcement by presuming everything would be fine and dandy in this town. Hemlock Creek may rarely have anything except minor crime, but everyone had a gun, and everyone had their breaking point. It simply took a raised voice and an end of a tether for a domestic disturbance to become a homicide.

* * *

Arthur LaFlamé stood in the middle of his living room. His mouth hung agape in shock and terror.

His 45 years on this earth had not prepared him for this nightmarish and surreal moment.

The walls around him were slicked with the bloody remains of the man who had broken into his home only an hour ago. The man's shredded clothes still clung to his strewn body parts, with the red fabric masking a lot of the blood that soaked into them.

"Damn," Arthur muttered under his breath. He stared into the open eyes of the severed head that now rested at his feet. With a red hat still firmly worn on it, and the once-white beard still framing a jolly grin, this head seemed still alive. As alive as it had been before, it was so viciously removed.

Arthur glanced down at his clothes. The spraying blood had covered his jumper and finely pressed pale trousers. As he felt the blood through his clothes pressing on his skin, Arthur then felt a wave of nausea.

Before tonight, Arthur had never believed in Santa Claus, not even as a child. But as he stood in this fictitious character's murdered remains, he fervently wished that he had always been right. He wished with all his might that Santa was still make believe and that he had somehow hallucinated the events of the evening.

This was *not* how he wanted to spend Christmas Eve.

A screeching cry caused Arthur to suddenly wince. He had hoped it was all over. He had hoped the murderous figure that massacred this man had left.

Nervously, Arthur moved his gaze from off the dead gift-giver, and behind him, toward the bay window overlooking the backyard. On the other side of these window's frost-covered glass, the blizzard beat down as heavy as it had done all week. Arthur wished it would pause so he could see if there was danger lurking out there. So he could escape. But he had no idea about anything. Not anymore.

Within a few seconds, a second screeching cry sounded out over the howls of the wind. Was it outside or in? He couldn't tell.

Springing into self-preservation mode, Arthur hurried across the room, over to the windows, and strained to focus outside. Between the icy flakes that beat down, he soon could make out what had happened.

He could see that same murderous cloaked figure now standing in his yard, with a large scythe in hand, cutting through one of the dozen reindeer that stood in front of a large wooden sleigh. The scream that Arthur had heard was the final pained cries of that poor animal. The scream before belonged to the first now-dead reindeer that lay in the snow.

This scythe that took their lives was the same weapon this thing had used to dispatch Santa. It was a terrifyingly large bladed implement, yet was one this figure seemed to use with great ease.

The two murdered reindeer now lay cloven in two with blood staining the snow around their freshly slaughtered bodies.

Tied in place in front of the empty sleigh, the rest of the dozen reindeer had no means of escape, not any way to fathom what was happening. They could only wait their turn as they neighed in confusion.

Pulling the bloodied scythe out of the snow, the figure then turned its attention toward them.

Arthur could not witness this anymore.

As he turned to run toward the staircase, the last words of the jolly dead man played over in his mind, spoken to the cloaked figure in an eerily calm yet joyful manner. "Please, brother, you don't have to do this."

As more of the reindeer's doomed wails drifted amongst the moaning gale, Arthur could only think of one thing; getting his gun. The last resort gun that he hid upstairs.

Reaching the first-floor landing, Arthur turned right and ran into the bedroom. Making a beeline for the bedside cabinet, he fumbled as he pulled open the drawer.

The terror he felt broke out of him in a cold sweat. His breathing became more and more erratic as he rushed. He could feel his heartbeat in his throat.

Inside the drawer, he reached for the bright yellow locked case that sat within. Nestled beneath the never-used box of condoms and a nearly empty box of tissues. This was a weapon he had never fired, nor even loaded, but was something that he was finally glad he had bought all those years ago.

The words of that strangely honest realtor hadn't deterred him from moving in. *This property isn't in the safest of neighborhoods*, she had said. Those words had quickly filled his mind with paranoia that at any moment his house would be set upon by looters, murderers, or rapists—all out to harm him. Despite that seemingly honest warning, any worry proved baseless. He had never had an iota of trouble since the day he picked up the keys. He felt safer here than in any other building he had lived in before. The gun he had purchased was, up until now, a clear waste of money. But tonight, tonight he was beyond glad he had it.

Pulling out the case with one hand, Arthur thrust his other into his trouser pocket and pulled out his house keys. Rifling through them, he couldn't see the only one he needed. The one to this lockbox.

Where was it?

As his eyebrows furrowed, Arthur dropped the case onto the bed and then searched his other pockets. Nothing.

As dread realization swamped Arthur, he gulped painfully. He could now see the key in his mind's eye. With a small yellow fob attached to it with the handwritten label saying 'security', he saw it. There on the sideboard in a bowl. Buried among all the other barely used keys.

The sideboard it sat on was next to the back door in the kitchen; the same one that now lay in shards on the floor. The same back door that the cloaked figure had broken in through.

Glimpsing himself in the floor-length bedroom mirror, Arthur regarded his scrawny frame. He looked from head to toe, from his prematurely bald head, over his pale and sickly skin, to his skinny legs.

What could I do? he thought to himself.

There was no sanity in someone like him trying

to fight a monster. There was nothing sensible about bringing any kind of fight to that half-goat/half-man thing that had proven its want for murder. Arthur knew full well that he had no chance of scaring the beast away, even *if* he could get those keys.

He closed his eyes as he tried to regain control of his breathing. Scenario after scenario played out in his mind's eye. Each one resulted in him meeting the sharp end of that creature's scythe.

So Arthur decided to do the one thing he knew he had to do.

He grabbed the telephone from the bedside cabinet, crouched down to the floorboards, backed up slowly, and crawled under the bed.

He resigned himself to what he saw as the best current option, to hide from the horror in the nearest place he could.

When he was fully under the bed, in its shadow, Arthur picked up the telephone and dialed 9-1-1.

He felt the pit of his stomach fall each time the rotary dial whirred loudly back into place.

"Emergency services. What is the nature of the emergency?" came the voice from the receiver.

Arthur froze. What was he going to say? He couldn't say that Santa had been killed in his house with a scythe. They would just hang up the phone on him, no doubt labeling it a prank call.

"Uh, I heard gunshots... Someone has a gun," was all he could think of to whisper into the phone.

* * *

Taking a step onto the porch, E pointed his gun ahead of him. He felt a weird sense that not only did he have to be prepared for anything, but he would probably be firing his gun today. The first time in many years.

Edging closer to the house's open front door, he shouted loudly, "This is Sheriff Eaves-Eagleton! Anyone in there with a gun or anything meaning to harm, I suggest you put it right down, right now. If ya shoot me, or try to attack me, you'll not only have the gas chamber in your future, you'll also get my wife. And most folks'll know better than to chance her anger!"

That may have sounded like a joke, but it was also true. No one got on the wrong side of Agnes Eaves-Eagleton and won. No one.

Peering down the hallway, E noticed the pool of blood on the hardwood floor that led into the living room.

"Goddamit," he mumbled under his breath. Now that there was blood, this was becoming more of a worst-case scenario for him. This was not a paranoid call from a nosey neighbor as he hoped.

Glancing back over his shoulder, he looked toward his patrol car. The rules stated that he should always call in for backup. It was clearly stated in the regulations that no officer should enter an unsafe area alone. But E could not face that storm again. Not yet. *To hell with the rules,* he thought.

Gripping the pistol tighter, E raised it to aim dead ahead.

"I'm coming in. Now don't any of ya think of tryin' anythin' stupid."

* * *

The seconds soon turned to minutes, and those minutes flitted by into an hour. Bit by bit, Arthur's panic had subsided, as he was hiding under the bed. The threat in the house had become less present the longer he silently hid. Despite this, his breathing remained stilted, but it no longer pushed him toward any hyperventilation, as it had chanced earlier. The sweat that had dripped down his body was now dried, leaving him in a slight chill.

As he shivered, his mind replayed for the hundredth time, all the events he had witnessed that evening. He re-questioned everything he had seen during each horrific moment.

Santa Claus? How could he be real? He couldn't, could he?

No. It had to be a man. A normal man wearing a red costume. After all, that red look was an invention that the Coca-Cola company created, *wasn't it?* His outfit should be green if he was the bona fide, real, honest-to-god, St. Nick. *Right?*

Yet, despite the attempts to convince himself

otherwise, he couldn't forget that he'd seen a sleigh pulled by reindeer, parked up in the backyard.

As Arthur quietly cowered underneath the bed, something was happening downstairs, something he had no clue about.

With a muted click, the front door had opened soon after Arthur had run upstairs. At first, nothing had entered except the gusts of the snowstorm. Gusts that elegantly blew their flakes into the house, spiraling to the hardwood floor as they fell. At first, the snow melted away, then as the hallway temperature fell, the snow soon settled inside.

The weather outside was building in its rage, beating down, heavier and heavier, onto all within Hemlock Creek.

Then, outside the house, as if birthed by the very storm itself, something small crawled along the frozen asphalt. Dragging itself out of the white squall, across the front lawn, and toward the now open door, was a pale creature. No bigger than a house cat, this thing used its long, clawed hands to pull its trailing body behind it. A trailing body that had no legs nor a tail; instead, it dragged a loose collection of fleshy tendrils that resembled thin, meaty tassels. With no eyes and no ears, this creature's face only had two slits for a nose and a wide-open mouth, packed with blackened, serrated teeth.

As this thing approached the porch, it

clambered up the two wooden steps and headed into the open house.

This creature, though, was far from alone.

Following its path from within the belly of the storm, dozens of identical creatures soon followed; dragging their monstrous forms into the warmth of the house, unbeknownst to the hiding Arthur.

These creatures all crawled forward blindly, focused on their destination, never once pausing or turning away as if they were drawn to the house, or more specifically, the living room.

The cacophony of Storm Hella's tempest, which screamed throughout the neighborhood, had masked these monster's arrival.

As the multitude of slithering terror clawed their way inside, one different creature trailed behind them. A much larger thing.

Standing around eight feet tall, this creature resembled the smaller ones; without eyes or ears, and its lower half was also a collection of loose hanging flesh. Yet instead of crawling on its belly, this larger monster impossibly floated a few inches off the ground; its hanging flesh dangled loosely in the air, undulating with the motion of this creature's movement.

In one of its taloned hands, this floating creature held an ancient-looking scroll, and in its other, a large black feathered writing quill.

It followed its smaller brethren and headed into the house.

* * *

The sheriff stepped carefully across the hallway, following the blood trail on the floor, toward the living room of 932 Amberson. This house had been open to the elements for a while and the sounds of the storm were deafening, even from inside the building.

Cautiously, E peered into the living room, pistol pointed at the ready.

He soon saw what awaited him; the red Santa outfit on the massacred remains of a man's body.

E's expression dropped.

"Dammit," he said. "Just what I fuckin' need."

A murder in Hemlock Creek.

A festive murder, no less.

* * *

It was another hour until Arthur summoned up enough courage to move out from underneath the bed. He had not been aware of the creatures that had come into the house. What with the cacophony emitted by the storm being so loud, he presumed that all the danger had passed. He had been under the bed for so long and heard nothing.

There were no more cries from any victims of its slaughter; no sounds at all.

No one had come looking for him, no one even came upstairs.

The murderous thing must have left. With this

sure though, Arthur decided that it was most assuredly safe for him to get the keys from the kitchen, and then free the gun from its locked case. He might not need it now that the creature had gone, but it would make him happier knowing he had protection at the ready.

His mind was busily awash with panicked reasoning, as he attempted to assert logic and common sense to what he witnessed.

He now considered himself foolish for having hidden under that bed at all. He realized that there was never any sign of danger toward him. In fact, there was no evidence that the scythed monster meant him any harm at all. It had just broken in, killed Santa, left, then killed the reindeer. Surely, if that beast wanted him dead, he would be.

He had just been caught in the middle, *right*? He was safe, *wasn't he*? Just stuck amid a battle he had no right to witness.

As Arthur thrust all remaining cowardice and fear far away from his conscious mind, he crawled out from under the bed and stood up.

Grabbing the gun case from on top of the bed, he gritted his teeth, steeling himself, then crept out of the room on tiptoes. Across the hallway, he silently moved over to the top of the staircase.

If it was not for the continuous howling of the storm outside, Arthur might have heard what was now happening on the floor below. He might have realized that he was *not* alone and chosen instead to remain hidden under the bed.

In the living room a few feet from him, the still levitating larger creature overlooked the work of the smaller creatures it commanded. With the scroll firmly in its grasp, the creature scrawled symbols with the quill. As the quill wrote, each blood-red mark faded on the paper for a few moments, as if magic. When the quill ran dry, the thing bent down and dipped the tip into one of the pools of blood below; refilling the ink before returning to mark down more disappearing symbols.

The smaller creatures were licking up the blood from the carpets and walls while also eating the chunks of gore left from the massacre. This was a demonic clean-up crew busily at work; one which also extended beyond this room and led into the backyard, where the tendrilled creatures feasted on the remains of the reindeer. Ravenous and without cessation, they ate and ate and ate all the evidence.

The large creature then paused its writing for a moment, as it observed the severed, smiling head on the floor beneath it. The jolly visage that stared up with dead, glassy eyes.

After a moment, the creature spoke with a cracked and strangled voice. "And a Merry Christmas to you," it said almost mockingly.

"Oh fuck no," came the whimpering voice from the hallway. An exclamation so weak that it might have been unheard by human ears. But for the creatures present, it was as clear as day.

Turning en masse, each thing in the house now

looked directly toward Arthur. Their expressions displayed their serrated teeth in wide and identical smiles. A disturbing and terrifying sight.

Urine streaked down the inside of Arthur's trousers as he remained frozen to the spot, petrified.

Despite the creatures having no eyes, Arthur could still sense each of them somehow staring at him. Pressure then built up inside him as bile crawled out of his stomach and slowly forced its way up his throat.

Gripping the handle of the gun case tighter, Arthur mustered all his strength, turned, then forced himself to run toward the kitchen, all whilst his mouth expelled a stomach full of vomit. The putrid matter fell from his lips, splattered down his clothing, and along the floor—marking his trail along to the kitchen sideboard.

Without time to wipe the chunks of stomach lining away from his lips, Arthur quickly lunged forward and rummaged in the bowl frantically until he found the needed key.

"Halt!" screamed the large floating creature, who now appeared in the hallway.

Arthur, beyond scared, turned to face it.

The thing's quill pointed threateningly toward Arthur.

With options of fight or flight, Arthur did not spend a single second considering unlocking the gun case and battling these things. The only consideration he had was to run as far away and as fast as he could.

With the key in one hand, and gun case in the other, Arthur sprinted through the open back door and into the backyard.

The escape from the house led him into not only the middle of the still-present blizzard, but also among the remnants of the reindeer massacre. Something he had forgotten about.

Stopping in his tracks as he approached the murder scene, Arthur quickly lost his footing on the ice and slipped forward.

The lock box he held slipped from his grasp, as his vomit-encrusted mouth loosed a panicked yelp.

The snowfall swirled from every direction but did little to shield his vision from seeing not only the decimated reindeer corpses but the small creatures that now covered them, consuming their flesh and bone.

As he scrambled to his feet, the creatures' attention—like the ones inside—now shifted toward him with the same serrated-toothed smile, plastered onto each of their surreal faces. As their lips widened in unison, blood from their feasting trickled out from between their monstrous teeth.

From the open doorway to the house, the large creature quickly emerged, still pointing its quill toward Arthur. It screamed its command at him once again. "Halt!"

Tearing himself away from the horror, Arthur quickly seized the fallen gun case and then clambered to his feet. He ran as fast as he could, away from the house, away from the horror. Deeper and deeper into the storm. He did not care where he was going. He just wished to be far away from here.

* * *

E was sitting back in the driver's side of his patrol car. Though now sheltered from the storm outside, he looked battered by the elements he'd just had to fight to get back from the house.

His mind, though, was not on the weather, but on what he had just witnessed inside 932 Amberson.

With his hand slightly trembling, he picked up the radio handset from its cradle and clicked on the button.

"Hey... Agnes?" he said with a tired drawl.

"What is it E? You ok?" came the reply over the speaker.

"Send everyone we got to Amberson." He rubbed his eyes with his thumb and forefinger as he struggled to keep his composure. Being this tired and needing to manage what was inside that house would take every fiber of his being to get through the night.

"You need a coroner?" Agnes said.

"Yeah. Wake Atkins, too," he replied. "Ain't trustin' Lorenzo on his own."

"How many were shot?" Agnes asked with some urgency in her voice.

"No guns, from what I can tell. But there's ...

Aw hell... Just get everyone down here. It's a goddamn mess."

Placing the handset back on its cradle, he then switched the radio off. He couldn't answer more questions, even from Agnes. Everyone would have to see it for themselves.

***

Arthur ran faster and faster through the torrential snowfall. The flakes blew at him from ahead, slowing his escape. Struggling to keep his footing as he sprinted, Arthur could not help but worry about the creatures.

He then remembered the phone call he had made to the police. *Shit*! He wondered whether he should call them back to warn them. *And say what? No.*

He thought better and decided to just save himself.

The police would no doubt see what had happened — suspect Arthur of course. Then, when they ran their tests, they would see he didn't do any of it. Science would prove his innocence. But until then... he would have to run.

Far behind—over the sounds of the icy gales encircling the streets, even over the cries of his lungs screaming for air—a roar pierced through the night and permeated the streets.

A roar of something now chasing him.

At now a full sprint, Arthur glanced over his shoulder.

He saw a flash of what was fast approaching, and his blood ran colder.

The thing that first came into the house had found him.

That cloaked figure was closing in, roaring furiously as it moved. Its hooves echoed on the snow-covered road beneath it. The scythe it brandished continually slashed the air in front of it, in large sweeping motions.

Another scream broke through the noise as Arthur cried his own roar, but his was one of extreme fear.

No wonder this thing had found him, he thought. He was running in the open streets.

But, as his bad luck would soon dictate, before he could change direction, Arthur was immediately plunged into the grasp of darkness as he collided, at speed, with the solid metal side of one of the street's many lamp posts.

* * *

With all of Hemlock Creek sheriff's department now on the scene, E—notebook in hand—walked from his patrol car through the falling snow, toward the crime scene inside 932 Amberson.

Ruing the loss of his hat, he kept an eye out as he approached the porch, hoping to spot it among the settled snow. He could hear the comments now: *Santa lost his hat, eh? At least you still got your sack!*

Getting to the open front door for the second time that night, E quickly stamped the snow off his boots and stepped inside. He dreaded to see what was in the living room once more. It wasn't like he hadn't seen a dead body before, but some crimes, crimes like this, were too horrific to easily forget. Scenes like this stayed with you long after the bodies had been buried.

"Sheriff?" came a voice from the living room. A voice that belonged to Doc. Atkins. "That you?"

"Yup," E replied wearily as he stepped around the corner of the hallway and into the murder scene. Two of E's deputies stood next to Atkins as he examined the dismembered remains of a large man in a Santa outfit.

Smiling to the sheriff, Atkins motioned to the severed head next to him. "Uncanny, ain't it?"

"Hmm?" said E.

"Santa," he said, pointing to the head, then pointing at E. "And another Santa! It's uncanny."

"Fuck you, Atkins." E grumbled in reply, "show some fucking respect."

Atkins held up his hands as his cocky smile dropped in a mock apology. "Sorry, I meant to say, Sheriff Santa. Gotta get those titles right."

Normally, this kind of comment would have been light-heartedly received by E, but he did not feel in a particularly jocular mood.

Atkins, though, had known the sheriff for

many years and could tell when enough really was enough. Changing the subject quickly, the doctor continued by asking, "What d'you think happened here?"

With a shrug, E glanced around the room, looking at the blood that coated most of the walls and the chunks of gore that had been scattered across the floor. "No goddam idea." He then glanced back at Atkins. "Where's Lorenzo?"

"That asshole's out back," the doctor replied. "Fucking up the crime scene, no doubt."

E chuckled as Atkins' comment caught him off-guard and allowed the horror of the scene to be forgotten for a split second.

"You two still ain't friends, huh?" E asked.

"Friends? With that dumb piece of shit?" Atkins sighed as he continued. "Can't fuckin' wait till he gets the fuck out of town."

"Lemme guess," E interjected. "Then after he goes, you can do this job to your highfalutin standards?" Before Atkins could think of a witty retort, E continued. "Now, aside from your love of our coroner, when do you think the time of death was?"

"Coroner Lorenzo Fucktard thought it was between 2 p.m. and 4 p.m."

"And lemme guess, that's wrong?" E asked, knowing full well it *was* wrong. It was *always* wrong.

Lorenzo had been a mistake that the Mayor had forced on the department for the past three years.

E's previous heart attack had forced him to take a six-month sabbatical from duties, during which time the Mayor had taken control and employed his unqualified nephew in the vacant position of coroner. But with all small-town politics, nothing was ever easy. E had no choice but to bide his time and ask Atkins to correct Lorenzo's work on every case, with the promise of getting the coroner's position as soon as Lorenzo was gone.

At least the mistakes Lorenzo made amounted to little in this town. It wasn't every day that the exact time of death or the proper processing of bodies meant that much when there were so few deaths in the town.

Firing Lorenzo would have normally happened after the first few mistakes, but the Mayor needed to be kept happy at all costs. E was, after all, lucky that the council still allowed him to be sheriff after his recovery. So, he had no choice then but to have everyone on his side.

Luckily for everyone, Lorenzo had less than a week to go before he moved to Utah. Then E and the Hemlock Creek police department would be free to employ Doc. Atkins to take his place.

"Rigor ain't even set in yet," Atkins said. "He died less than 3 hours ago, same with the ones outside."

Taking his pencil, E noted down the information in his notebook, then asked, "You see any trace of any bullets?"

"Nope," replied the doctor. "You were right

with that. No evidence of gunfire anywhere. This was all done with a large blade. Machete or ax or somethin' like that."

E grimaced at the severed head on the floor. "Poor bastard," he grumbled.

"I can tell you now, this wasn't quick either. This took a lot of rage and a *lot* of determination."

"I'll say it again. Poor bastard," E repeated under his breath.

"The worst thing about it is, I found traces of what I think is semen and feces..." Atkins' words quickly trailed off as his attention moved from E and into the hallway.

"Arthur?" the doctor exclaimed. "What in fuck?"

Turning, E's eyes widened as he saw the man he knew as Arthur LaFlamé standing there naked, stained head to foot in blood. Staring back. Terrified. Holding a plastic case in one of his hands.

"Oh fuck no!" Arthur screamed at them, as he then turned and bolted out of the smashed open back door.

"Arthur! Stop!" E shouted as he ran after him.

Outside, Arthur tumbled down the steps into the backyard, and crumpled into a heap, just in front of Lorenzo and some deputies who now examined the scene. Each of them turned in surprise at the naked man's arrival.

"Stop!" E called out again.

But Arthur didn't listen and scrambled to his feet, then ran into the thick storm.

Turning with a look of annoyance toward his men, E barked, "Why the hell didn't you try to stop him?"

Getting no answer and only blank stares, E quickly pulled the gun from his holster and made chase after Arthur.

* * *

Slowly coming back from his unconsciousness, Arthur blinked rapidly, staring up at the lamppost he had collided so violently against.

The snow had settled deep on him. He wondered how long he had been there. Whether he had lost the monster on his trail?

Lifting himself into a sitting position, he gritted his teeth as a sharp pain shot through his head. Holding a hand up to his scalp, he winced as his fingers touched a fresh, deep, and bloody wound along his temple.

He was injured, yet was still alive. That was all that mattered. The injury would heal, even though it was a pain so intense that it blurred his vision.

Despite the agony, he closed his eyes and smiled to himself.

Yet...

Something was different.

Something was not right.

His smile soon faded as he realized that.

He was cold.

Too cold.

Looking down, he saw that he was now naked. Not only that, but he was also covered in dried blood.

"What the hell?" he said under his breath.

He turned and saw the gun case, now open. The key now firmly in its lock. He then noticed that in his hand sat the gun. And it was still smoking.

Without a beat passing, a slow, rhythmic clack of hooves on asphalt sounded from behind him.

Before Arthur could scream in protest, he had no time to move as the monster's scythe swung through the air and pierced through his back.

The ancient, blackened blade then burst through his stomach with such force that it yanked Arthur's body forward. The blade sliced through the metal lamppost in front of him. Pinning Arthur's naked, near-to-death body against it.

As Arthur gurgled a moan with one of the last breaths in his body, the half-man/half-goat-creature opened its heavy robe. From inside its clothing, within the darkness, emerged four sets of charred corpse arms. Four bodies then clambered out from inside this creature's darkness and grabbed onto the now-dying Arthur.

These four hellish beings soon surrounded him as he struggled to breathe; the scythe having sliced through his lungs, forcing his own blood to slowly drown him.

The two smaller beings were the first to attack as they lunged forward and viciously clawed into

Arthur's flesh. They were soon joined in their attack by the two larger beings.

Arthur, still embedded in the lamppost with the scythe, was then slowly ripped apart as the half-man, half-goat-creature looked on, laughing.

Despite his concerted attempts, Arthur could not make even a single sound. Blood smothered his voice as the flesh was ripped from his body.

It was during these last few moments that Arthur's mind flooded with the vision of him standing outside the house he used to own. The house at 932 Amberson.

Staring in through the bay window he watched as his ex-wife and two daughters, all of whom were dressed up as reindeer, sat on the couch. They were celebrating the festive season with Donald Eckwiss, his ex-wife's new husband, who was dressed up as Santa Claus.

Arthur saw himself being consumed by a blinding rage as he broke through the back door, armed with an old machete he used to use for gardening. A machete his wife had taken in their divorce, along with everything else. She had even taken his gun, which she kept in the same bedside cabinet he had done. But no restraining order would stop him from exacting his revenge on those who had betrayed him.

Dangerous and unstable, his wife had labeled him to the court.

Arthur felt the rage not only toward her, and to the man who stole his place, but he also felt this unbridled rage toward his daughters. If they didn't want him in their lives, they would have no lives left to live.

Arthur's dying vision then showed him surprising them in the living room, whilst they were in the middle of playing charades. He saw himself beheading Donald. He then saw his wife and daughters scream as they tried to escape, yet didn't make it any further than ten feet out back before his rage took them, too.

In the last blinking moments of his life, Arthur then saw himself debasing their bodies by chopping them all into small pieces, stripping himself naked, and then debasing their remains further.

He now, for his last moment, remembered all that he'd done.

And he felt sick with remorse. He hoped they could forgive him in heaven. Though as he felt himself being ripped to shreds, he presumed that heaven was not his destination.

* * *

With the blizzard now stopped, and the morning sun breaching the horizon, the town stood silent.

Agnes, dressed in an oversized police jacket, stood by the police vehicle as she waited for the deputies to return. E had not returned from when he chased Arthur LeFlamé.

"He'll be fine," Atkins assured her, placing his

hand on her shoulder. "He's one strong bastard of a man."

"He *better* be fine," she replied, fighting back the tears as she dreaded the worst-case scenario. "Or I'll kill him."

Atkins smiled.

Ahead of them, Lorenzo was standing by his car smoking a cigarette as the deputies carried out the body bags. Not wanting to take any attention away from E, Atkins kept all angry comments about the coroner to himself.

"Why didn't anyone stop him? He's got a heart condition." Agnes asked.

"No idea. At least it stopped snowing. That's something, right?" Atkins thought it best to illustrate some positives.

"Doc," said a voice from behind them. Atkins and Agnes turned to see a deputy walking toward them. In his hand, he held E's police hat. "I found this."

Agnes's heart sank.

It was another twenty minutes until her fears could be dispelled; when she would hear the happy, relieved shouts of "We found him, he's alive!"

* * *

E lay in the middle of the sidewalk, his heart having punished him for the second time in his life. His health failed to win, yet again. His attempts to chase Arthur had proved too much for his body to take, and he had paid the price. Though not the final one.

Some deputies now stood around him. They had informed him that Arthur's body had been found on the next street over, having shot himself in the head.

As E lay in the snow, glad it was over, he considered his mortality. Yet he knew this was not his time. He would not be taken away at Christmas, of all times. Not from Agnes. She wouldn't allow it. No god would be foolish enough to invoke her wrath, especially at her favorite time of year.

He then heard words he wanted to hear more than the sirens of an ambulance.

"E, Agnes is here."

It was only a few moments later that he lost consciousness and heard his wife calling out his name through her tears.

"Eeeeeeeeee!"

* * *

The following afternoon in the hospital, when E came to, Agnes would let him have it. She would shout and scream at him for bringing this all on himself. But for now, in the darkness of his sleep, he smiled happily that she was nearby.

* * *

Arthur stood in the middle of his living room. Again.

His mouth was agape. Again.

His 45 years on this earth had not prepared him for this moment. It never did. And this Christmas would play out over and over for eternity.

Arthur would never be forgiven, nor would he ever be allowed to forget.

And in the brief moments of his hellish death, he accepted this fate.

He knew he deserved every single moment of it.

Eleven Twisted Christmas Songs

You may ask yourself, what the hell is this all about then? That is a valid question. The short answer is, I do not know. The long answer is, I wrote these for a cancelled anthology years ago. I found them whilst compiling content for this collection, and they made me chuckle. But I have no idea why I am including them here, aside from they link to the festive feel of the last story, and maybe they will make you smile too.

I

Jingle Bells
Corpses smell
Underneath the floor
Incense, candles, potpourri cannot mask the gore
Hey
Jingle Bells
Corpses smell

A strange noise now does sound
As those you killed do return,
from their rest underground

II

Good King Wenceslas looked out
On the feast he would eat
Bodies piled up high and wide
Lots of blood and fresh meat
Brightly shone the moon that night
Big and round and full
Now Wenceslas was not a man
But a cruel werewolf

III

Twas the night before Xmas
and all through the streets
The dead were stirring
and looking for meat
The people hid in their homes boarded tight
As the dead waited patiently, night after night

IV

Silent Night, Final Night
All now calm, all was bright
In the blast, all life was crushed
All that breathed now bone and dust
Rest in atomic glow

Rest in atomic glow

V

Hark! The herald demons sing,
"Glory to the old god king!
Death on earth and mercy forfeit,
Burn the humans in the pit."
Joyful, all ye devils rise,
Join the triumph, burn the skies,
With demonic host proclaim:
"Dagon rises once again."
Hark! The herald demons sing,
"Glory to the old god king!

VI

A babe in a manger
Now the living dead
This little lord Jesus's parents had fled
Now crying alone, he craved for fresh brains
But only a baby, had no teeth to maim.

VII

Rudolph the Red-Nosed Reindeer
Had a very slick wet nose
T'was the blood of victims
he had ate from head to toe
All of the other reindeer
had no chance to run and flee

As Rudolph the Red-Nosed Reindeer
Had killed them all in their sleep

VIII

We three beasts of darkness are
Baring teeth like jaguar
Hearts and elbows, heads and leg bones
Eating them near and far
We three beasts, we three beasts

IX

I just want your heart for Christmas
It is the one small thing I still need
I'll bury the remains of you
Underneath the Christmas tree
I just want your bloody heart
More than you could ever know
Make my spells come true
All I want for Christmas is you... dead

X

Hark how the knife
Sweet silver knife
Cuts thru your heart
Rips you apart
Darkness is here
Bringing no cheer
To young and old

Meek and the bold
Slice-Cut, Slice-Cut
That is the song
With painful ring
All screaming (ARGH, URRRH, ARGH)

XI

The moon is full
The spirits rise
We're here tonight
All flesh and flies
Simply ending your wonderful Christmastime
You party on
Yet, you should fear
As we now gift
your screams and tears
Simply ending your wonderful Christmastime

ALSO BY CHRISTIAN FRANCIS

<u>Novels</u>

Wishmaster - The Novelisation

Everyday Monsters: The Animus Chronicles 1

Titan Find (AKA Creature) - The Novelisation

Incubus: The Descent: The Animus Chronicles 2

Vamp - The Novelisation

The Dead Woods

Killing Frank (with Tom Holland)

<u>Novellas</u>

The Sacrifice of Anton Stacey

<u>Graphic Novels</u>

Hellraiser: Anthology Vol 1 & 2

Hellraiser: Bestiary Vol 4 & 6

<u>Other</u>

Anti-Rule: Navigating The Lies About Fiction Writing

Hellbound and Damned: Three Screenplays